THE SPIRIT IS WILLING

THE SPIRIT IS WILLING

by Betty Baker

MACMILLAN PUBLISHING CO., INC.
NEW YORK
COLLIER MACMILLAN PUBLISHERS
LONDON

Macmillan Publishing Co., Inc.
866 Third Avenue, New York, N.Y. 10022
Collier Macmillan Canada Ltd.

Library of Congress catalog card number: 73-8576
Printed in the United States of America

3   4   5   6   7   8   9   10

Library of Congress Cataloging in Publication Data

Baker, Betty. The spirit is willing.

[1. United States—Social life and customs—1865-1918—Fiction]
I. Title.
PZ7.B1693Sp   [Fic]   73-8576   ISBN 0-02-708270-9

*To Carries of every age
and every era*

Contents

1

Apache Sam's Skedaddle

Portia said, "We could wash our hair."

Without looking up from the magazine on her lap Carrie said, "We did that day before yesterday."

Besides, Mrs. Dollingwood's copy of *Frank Leslie's Weekly* had arrived on yesterday's stage and Carrie didn't want to do anything until she'd read the last installment of "Heroes of the Bastille." She'd reached a place where the heroine was pining and reflecting. Until she came to something interesting Carrie could give half her attention to Portia's chatter.

"But here's a recipe for hair rinse." Portia read

from *Godey's Ladies' Book*, "It will add luster and radiance to your tresses and capture admiring glances wherever you stroll."

"What's in it?"

"Castor oil and whiskey scented with lavender water."

"We'd probably smell like a saloon. Besides, where would we get the whiskey?"

Portia gave an exasperated, "Oh, Carrie," and turned the page. "Look, an afternoon gown with a train. Isn't it elegant? I wish I was old enough for long skirts."

"I don't. They're hot and dusty and trip you up. Besides, then you have to wear corsets and you can't ever sit comfortable."

"You shouldn't sit like that anyhow. It's a most unladylike posture."

Carrie was sitting cross-legged on the porch floor, her skirts stretched between her knees to make a resting place for the magazine. Portia sat on the top step, her skirts arranged properly over her legs.

"A lady is circumspect at all times," she said.

The cactus shadows on the front yard were almost short enough for noon. Carrie figured she had lots of time to practice being a lady but not much left before she had to go home. All the same, she scrooched forward to sit beside Portia and tugged her skirt toward her shoe tops before returning to her reading. Tracing the lines of small type with her finger, she was soon lost in the strangeness of Paris.

Portia jabbed her in the ribs. "Look who's coming."

Carrie caught the smell of wet desert and the thud of horse hooves. Without raising her eyes she said, "The water sprinkler."

"But look who's driving!"

Carrie marked her place with a finger and looked. It was only Frank Ainsley.

He'd been hanging around the saloons and hotels on Main Street since the Four Paws Circus had left Stringtown in January. Carrie sometimes used him as a bad example to her younger brother Buzzer. They were both on the lookout for make-a-million schemes, but where Buzzer worked hard at his silly notions, riding a water sprinkler around town would be Frank Ainsley's idea of hard labor. Carrie wondered if he planned to sell some of the water on his own. The Chinese on the other side of town had hard work carrying enough for their laundries and gardens.

She frowned. "I wonder what happened to Apache Sam. He was driving early this morning. Willie and Buzzer hitched a ride with him."

"He probably went to join Geronimo." Portia got to her feet and leaned against a porch post, arranging herself like a picture in *Godey's Ladies' Book*. All she needed was a tennis racquet or a golf stick. As the huge barrel wagon neared the house, spraying water from both sides, she sang out, "Hello, Mr. Ainsley."

The young man on the driver's seat shifted the

reins into one had so he could raise his black derby with the other. "Morning, Miss Portia. Miss Carrie."

Carrie called out, "Where's Apache Sam?"

"That Injun declared himself a holiday, Miss Carrie. I volunteered my services out of a deep concern for our fair but dusty town."

Then he'd better drive slower, the way Apache Sam did, and let the street get properly wet. Carrie also noticed there were no boys following the wagon. Even on days the new ice wagon delivered there were always two or three boys around the sprinkler, dodging in and out of the sprays. Frank Ainsley must have chased them away. Apache Sam never did. It wasn't that he couldn't. Willie said the Indian spoke English good as anybody in Stringtown and better than some.

The wagon lurched past, water darkening the dirt street.

Portia called after it, "You certainly add elegance to that old wagon, Mr. Ainsley."

Carrie snorted. The black suit and checkered vest were better than Apache Sam's ragged clothes, but she wouldn't call them elegant.

Frank Ainsley tipped his derby and bowed. "Why, thank you, Miss Portia."

Portia sighed, watching the wagon go down the street and around the corner. "Don't you admire the way he says Poah-shyah? There's nothing like a Southern gentleman."

"Frank Ainsley's no gentleman. Buzzer says he lives upstairs in the Rough-n-Ready Saloon."

Portia struck a pose and quoted from one of her recitations, " 'His haunt . . . his den . . . his anything but home!' What Frank Ainsley needs is a home and family. The love of a good woman."

Carrie lost her place in the magazine. "Why, Portia Dollingwood! Frank Ainsley must be all of twenty years old. You're only fourteen."

"I'd look sixteen if Mama let me put my hair up." She pushed her long hair up from her neck. "Do I look regal?"

"You look like Mrs. Hokelander playing the harlot in the Easter morality play."

Portia stuck out her tongue and went to sit in the porch swing. Carrie wondered if the sun was getting to her. Portia had never spent a summer in the desert before. As soon as school let out, Portia's mother always took her to San Francisco, but in May, Geronimo had broken out of the reservation. Mr. Dollingwood refused to let his wife and daughter make the day-long stagecoach ride to the railroad while Apaches were raiding. Carrie was secretly grateful to Geronimo. When Portia was gone, she had no place to go to get away from home.

Portia reclined in a corner of the swing, closed her eyes and crossed her arms on her breast. "I'm the Lily Maid of Astolat floating down the river on my bier."

Carrie said, "I suppose Frank Ainsley is Lancelot," and was immediately sorry. Portia sometimes got carried away with her Dramatic Recitations. A few weeks back she'd been mad Ophelia for three days. Carrie didn't want her going into a decline from unrequited love. Portia might worry her father into sending her to San Francisco, Apaches or no Apaches.

Quickly Carrie added, "Anyways, that poem is silly. Nobody would float a corpse down a river on a raft."

"Oh, Carrie!"

"Well, they wouldn't. It would capsize or get snagged and waterlogged. Even if it didn't, the turkey buzzards and the ravens would start. . . ."

"Carrie!" Portia clapped her hands over her ears.

Carrie hunched over her magazine. "Well, they would."

Portia took her hands down and sighed. "Really, Carrie, you have no romantic sensibilities."

"I do, too. I'm as romantic as anybody."

"I'm the Lily Maid of Astolat," Portia repeated. "My gown is finest lawn and the porch swing's twined with roses."

"It's too late to start a theatrical," Carrie reminded her.

"I weary of plays." Portia sat up. "Plays are but shadows." She got to her feet and raised her right hand in the pose of Declaration.

"It is time we tasted life, real life. Life with its sorrow." She did the pose, head bent into the curve of her arm. "Life with its fear." She did Dread, hands pushing to one side, head turned away.

If she was going to run through every pose in *The Art of Dramatic Recitation*, Carrie had time to finish the serial. She found her place and read almost a column before Portia plunked down on the swing and declared, "I wish they'd hurry and catch Geronimo! What is there to *do*?"

"There's the Fourth of July. It's about the biggest celebration Stringtown has."

"That's more than two weeks yet."

"And there's Emma Lou Smedley's entertainment."

Portia made a face. "Making rosettes for the Fourth of July, followed by lotto. Besides, that isn't until tomorrow night."

"Tonight you're coming to my house."

There was a meeting of the Stringtown Shakespeare and Literary Society. Both their parents belonged. Carrie had to tend her brothers and Portia was going to spend the night.

"We could wash our hair," Carrie suggested. "Maybe Buzzer can get us some whiskey and we can try that hair rinse."

"We can smuggle it in after dark. Contraband. Spoils of war." Portia was just getting started when her mother opened the front door.

"Carrie," said Mrs. Dollingwood, "you must excuse Portia this afternoon. Mary wants the afternoon off after all and I'll need Portia's help serving refreshments."

"Yes, ma'am." Carrie knew she was being told to go home, but she wasn't going to move until Portia did.

Portia waited until the door closed behind her mother, then made a face. "At least it's something to do."

Carrie suspected Portia really liked dressing up and passing silver trays to the ladies. "What meeting is it?"

"Ladies of the Library."

"Maybe you'll hear something interesting."

Portia picked up as much news at her mother's afternoon meetings as Buzzer did selling newspapers, and she didn't have to be bribed to tell it.

Portia said, "They wait to tell the interesting things when I'm out of the room."

"What about the time Doc Brewster's sister dressed like a man and had him take her to the Gilded Cage?"

Portia laughed. "They couldn't wait to tell that. I still don't understand why she did it."

"I do."

"Carrie Thatcher! The Gilded Cage is a dance hall."

"It has a stage. People come from the East to play there."

"Nice women don't go in the Gilded Cage."

"Miss Brewster did."

Portia giggled. "Wasn't that scandalous? Remember how she had to cut her visit short and return to Philadelphia?"

"Yes." Carrie thought it terrible that Miss Brewster had been made to leave.

More cheerful, Portia said, "Maybe I will hear something today."

She pushed herself from the swing and began to gather the magazines. Carrie held on to *Frank Leslie's Weekly*, reading until the last possible moment.

"Take it with you," said Portia.

"Your mother hasn't read it yet." Mrs. Dollingwood was generous about lending her magazines but she liked to read them herself first.

"With a meeting this afternoon and another tonight, she won't have time to read. You can give it to me tonight."

"You go ask her first."

Portia went inside and was soon back with the magazine. "Mama said be careful of it and give it to me tonight."

"Tell her thank you and I'll take good care of it." She carried her treasure down the steps and the rock-lined path.

"See you tonight," called Portia.

"Come early," Carrie told her.

The dark color left by the sprinkler had faded. Carrie scuffed dust as she crossed the street. Portia's house had neighbors but Carrie's house stood alone. Her father had bought all the lots on that side of the block, planning to sell them when the town grew. With the windows closed and draped against the sun, the house looked deserted. The rose bushes bordering the front porch were wilty and dust-covered. This was the only planting done around the Thatcher house, partly because watering was a monstrous chore and partly because of the boys.

They'd worn the side and back yards bare. A few clumps of ocotillo remained, none of the thin, branchless stems more than knee-high. All longer ones had been used for arrows or lances. No cactus had survived four years of playing Indian to the boys' cavalry charges. Only the mesquite tree had grown, the ground under it packed stone hard.

Buzzer and Willie roosted in its crooked branches. Lonnie squatted in its pale shade, carefully piling kindling into a square.

"Look, Carrie," he yelled. "Look! Look at my corral."

Without detouring to look, Carrie told him, "That's fine."

Buzzer hung upside down from a branch. "When are we going to eat?"

"When Father comes home."

"He isn't coming home today. He went out to the mine. Tell Mother I'm starving."

"Starving," repeated Lonnie. "We're starving."

Willie just smiled at her. Carrie smiled back. The wonder wasn't that Willie and Buzzer were brothers but that they could stick together day and night and stay as different as sweet and sour.

The Thatcher back porch was as shady as Portia's

front one. Where the sun seldom reached, a large wooden box stood on rough timber legs. Two sides were covered with burlap, which was kept wet. The desert breeze passed through it, picked up the moisture and cooled the food kept inside, just as drinking water was cooled by wetting the burlap that was wrapped around the unglazed jar hanging from the ceiling.

Carrie stopped for a drink, pouring what remained in the dipper over the jar sacking. She felt the cloth on the cooler. Estrella was supposed to keep it soaked when she was working. She tried to forget it when she had the afternoon off, leaving it for Carrie to do. The sacking was nearly dry.

Carrie stomped inside, blinking against the heat and dimness of the kitchen. Her mother stood at the stove frying meat and potatoes.

"Where's Estrella?" Carrie asked her.

"She wanted to leave early. It's some saint's day."

"You let her go?"

Mrs. Thatcher fanned herself with a towel. "When she's raising her own family there won't be any time off for fiestas. Let her have it now."

"But we haven't had dinner." Carrie saw her entire afternoon vanishing in Estrella's undone chores as well as her own. "Damnation!"

Her mother whirled on her. "Carrie Thatcher, one more word like that and you'll stay in this house for a week."

Carrie wouldn't mind, not if she could read. But her mother noticed the magazine in her hand and added, "And if I catch you reading before your chores are done, I'll ask Mrs. Dollingwood not to lend you any magazines for a month. Now put on an apron and help me."

Carrie put the magazine on the dining room sideboard. With her mother in a genuine tizzy, Carrie had no intention of being caught reading. She'd have to be extra careful.

2

Greasy Dan's Sale

The only light came through knotholes and the gaps between sun-dried boards. It was scarcely enough to read by but Carrie didn't dare hold the door open to get more light. The privy could be seen from the back of the house and Mother had guessed that Carrie came out just to read, especially when there were chores to do.

Carrie hunched over *Frank Leslie's Weekly*. She waved flies from her face but was no more conscious of them than of the smell. She was back in the French Bastille waiting for rescue.

A fist pounded the door. Carrie jumped.

"Carrie, you in there? Hurry up!" It was Buzzer's voice, impatient and careless. "You really doing something or you just reading?"

Carrie sighed. She closed the magazine, stood up, lifted the hook and swung open the door. As she stepped out, Buzzer made a grab for the magazine.

"Not this one!" Carrie raised it out of his reach. "This is Mrs. Dollingwood's. It just came in on yesterday's mail."

"You was reading." Buzzer grinned up at her. "What did Mother say about that?"

Carrie stared down at his bare feet. "What did Mother say about going barefoot?"

"That I'll get snake bit or cactus stuck," he said cheerfully. He scooted into the privy and banged the door shut behind him.

Hiding the magazine in the fold of her skirt, Carrie strolled toward the house. Willie sat under the mesquite tree waiting for Buzzer. He scrooched around trying to hide four canning jars and a mop pail. One of the jars held the giant click beetle that had helped to ruin Carrie's day.

From the holes in Lonnie's big toe and the way he'd carried on, Mother had thought he was snake bit. The click beetle, hidden in the woodpile, had just caught the toe in its pincers hard enough to dent and break the skin. By morning it wouldn't even be sore, but Lonnie had screamed and cried until he'd made himself sick. Mrs. Thatcher was tending him, leaving supper preparations to Carrie.

More to put off peeling potatoes than from interest, Carrie said, "What are you doing with the beetle?"

"We're going to use it," Willie told her.

"What for?"

"Willie!" Buzzer must have cracked the door open because his voice wasn't muffled. He couldn't have known Carrie was still around because he yelled, "Go get one of those poles from the drying yard."

Carrie yelled back, "Did Mother say you could have it?"

"None of your beeswax!"

Carrie grinned. The summer before, Buzzer had figured that since his mother only used her washtubs and boards on Monday he could rent them to the Chinese laundrymen the rest of the week. A phrenologist had been in Stringtown reading people's futures by the bumps on their heads but Father had said he didn't need a reading to know that Buzzer had a well-developed Bump of Business. Mother said it was disgraceful and nothing to brag about. Carrie didn't think she'd like Buzzer having one of her clothesline props.

Willie scrambled to obey his brother. Carrie would have tried to worm more out of him but her mother called from the back door, "Carrie, have you finished the potatoes?"

"Not yet." She hadn't expected her mother to leave Lonnie so soon.

"Then get to them, please."

"Yes, Mother." She couldn't resist calling back to the privy, "We're eating supper early tonight, Buzzer, so you and Willie get yourselves back here."

Her younger brothers never had to do a cussed thing. Lonnie was only five, but when he was ten or twelve he wouldn't be expected to do any more than Willie and Buzzer, just carry in stove wood and chop kindling once in a while.

Tom, her older brother, had a real job back in New York City with the company that owned one of the biggest mines in town, the same one Father worked for. Carrie envied Tom more than any of the others, even more than Essie who no longer had to help around the house. She'd married a cavalry lieutenant and gone off to live with the Indians. Now that Geronimo was on the warpath, though, Essie might be having more excitement than Tom. Carrie stopped to consider the two situations.

No, she'd rather be with Tom. She could see an Indian any day but she'd never seen a trolley or a telephone or a building more than two stories high, really more than two stories high, not just two with a false front like some buildings along Main Street.

Holding the magazine behind her and hoping Mother wouldn't see, she by-passed the porch steps and went around the shady side of the house. The dining room windows and drapes would soon be opened in the hope that air from the shaded side would cool the room for supper. But the parlor windows and drapes were opened only for cleaning or company. Carrie headed for the second parlor window.

Almost under it was the water barrel, filled twice a week from the sprinkler. The water piped from the mountain to the kitchen sink was too expensive to use on Mother's roses.

Carrie pushed a rock to the barrel and climbed up. By kneeling on the barrel top she could open the parlor window. She lowered the magazine behind the drape, standing it on edge. The heavy green velvet held it upright against the wall.

A dining room window opened. Drapery rings clicked as Mother rearranged the drapery folds. Carrie ducked under the open window, hoping the ones on the back porch hadn't been opened first. They hadn't. She plunked down on the top step, home free, took a potato from the big pot at her side and peeled it before the windows behind her opened.

"Are you finished?" asked her mother.

Carrie swished the peeled potato in a bowl of water and dropped it in the pot of water at her feet. "Not yet." She chose another potato from the big pot at her side. "How's Lonnie?"

"Better. I told him he had to come down for supper. Why do these things always happen on Estrella's afternoon off?"

Carrie swished another potato. "He better not expect me to baby him tonight."

But her mother was gone from the window. She

came out to sit by Carrie, a knife in her hand. She flapped the front of her dress to cool herself.

"Each summer gets hotter." She sighed and reached for a potato. "And it's only June."

"It's cooler outside than in, especially in the shade. Why don't we cook out here in the summer?" Carrie gestured with her knife. "We could build a shade roof right over there for the stove and eat here on the porch."

"We are not going to live like heathen Indians."

"But it would be cooler."

"We are civilized people and we are going to live in a proper, civilized manner." Mrs. Thatcher took the pot on her lap and began cutting the peeled potatoes into pieces.

Carrie handed the last potato to her mother. "I bet Essie doesn't cook in a hot kitchen."

"She certainly does. An officer's wife must set a good example. Honestly, Carrie, where do you get these notions?" She stood up, the pot in her hands. "I'll get these on the stove. Oh, I need wood. The boys forgot."

"Again," said Carrie, but her mother was inside the house. If she'd heard, she'd have made some excuse for Buzzer. Boys got away with blue murder.

Carrie poured the potato washing water over the cooler, dividing it expertly along the tops of the two curtains. She'd been only a few years older than Lonnie when Essie had passed her the job of keeping the sacking wet. Carrie had been proud of the job then. Now she was sick and tired of it. She wished they had an icebox like the Dollingwoods.

She took the bowl and pot inside, dumped the peelings into the garbage bucket next to the sink, set bowl and pot on the table for washing and headed outside for the woodpile. She stepped inside the drying yard to check the number of clothesline props leaning against the high wooden fence. Five. There should have been six.

Carrie grinned and went for the wood, turning each piece over to check for scorpions and centipedes before picking it up. She saw Willie and Buzzer down in the dry stream where the garbage was dumped. They seemed to be digging with Mother's clothesline prop. Carrie couldn't imagine why. She'd have liked a closer look but there wasn't time.

Meeting nights meant early supper, but Lonnie hadn't let Mother get an early start. Everything had to be done at once. Carrie darted in and out, setting the dining room table, slicing bread, carrying from cooler to kitchen to dining room. Father came home and Lonnie came downstairs to brag about the monster bug. It kept him in the sitting room, out from underfoot.

Sliding wooden doors closed the parlor from the dining room. Carrie had hoped to sneak in and read but she didn't dare. She put the coffee on to boil and mashed potatoes while Mother creamed peas and fried meat. Buzzer and Willie raced through the kitchen, almost upsetting Carrie with a platter of steaks. They pounded down the hall and up the stairs to wash and comb. They were back down and at the table before Carrie got the coffee poured.

She slid into her seat opposite them. Father asked the blessing, and platter and dishes were passed. Mrs. Thatcher served Lonnie, then handed the dishes over his head to Carrie who had to find room for them again on the table. There was little time for talk. They were almost ready for dessert when Mrs. Thatcher said, "The water barrel wasn't filled today, Father. The rose bushes need washing off but I was afraid I wouldn't have enough water for tomorrow."

Mention of the water sprinkler usually brought Father's long complaint about boondoggling. The sprinkler hauled water pumped from the Marshall Mine. Mr. Marshall claimed he wasn't charging for the water, just for use of the sprinkler which was owned by the Marshall Freighting Company. Father claimed Marshall charged the town council enough to buy ten sprinklers and no matter what he called it he was selling water that had to be pumped out anyhow to keep the mine working.

Carrie figured most of her father's grumbling was because the company mine he managed also pumped out water but had to run it off into the desert. Then he had to pay tax for water from the Marshall Mine, Stringtown's largest. The company mine was smaller and drier, but any talk of the flooding mines made Carrie uneasy.

Hoping to head off Father's usual speech, Carrie said, "Frank Ainsley drove the sprinkler today. Something must have happened to Apache Sam."

"I hope he isn't sick." Mrs. Thatcher frowned at Buzzer and Willie. "The boys ride with him. It might be catching."

Mr. Thatcher said, "He was well enough to get out of town. On foot, too. Just walked off. Good thing he didn't take the horses. Marshall would've had the town council pay for them, too."

Quickly Carrie said, "I guess he went off to join Geronimo."

Willie shook his head.

Mrs. Thatcher said, "You never know, do you? He seemed so nice to Willie and now he's gone off to murder people in their beds."

"He isn't." It was Willie's voice.

They all stared at him. He flushed and swallowed hard, looking as if he had more to say, but Buzzer didn't wait for him.

"It was the mummy," Buzzer told them. "He didn't like the mummy."

3

Miss Brewster's Talking

All eyes turned on Buzzer.

He said, "Greasy Dan found an old mummy while he was prospecting. He brought it in today and sold it to T. Jay for a grubstake from Jenkin's Mercantile."

Carrie leaned forward. "What kind of mummy is it? Where did he find it? What does it look like?"

"Bundle of rags was all I saw." Buzzer wiped his plate clean with a crust of bread. "Didn't look much bigger than Lonnie, though."

His mother interrupted. "Buzzer, have you and Willie been inside that saloon?"

Carrie knew Buzzer had. He sold newspapers in the saloons every afternoon, leaving Willie outside to watch for Mother and her friends. That's when Willie had started talking to Apache Sam, who sat on the boardwalk between sprinkler rides. Carrie had kept silence to hold something big over Buzzer, but it had gone on so long that if Mother found out, Carrie would catch as much blame as Buzzer. She tried to look unconcerned and kept a worried eye on Willie. Not only couldn't Willie lie, he looked guilty when someone else did.

Buzzer said innocently, "Greasy Dan had to unpack it from his burro."

Willie went on drawing in his mashed potatoes and gravy as if he hadn't heard.

"Besides, Mr. Weatherberry wrote the mummy up for the *Epithet*," Buzzer continued. "It's all in the newspaper, how the mummy was brought in and how it'll be on display in the Rough-n-Ready starting Saturday."

Mr. Thatcher laughed. "That should earn Weatherberry a free drunk."

"Henry!" Mrs. Thatcher carried empty vegetable dishes to the kitchen, giving her daughter a don't-just-sit-there look.

Moving lazily, Carrie went around the table gathering silverware and stacking plates.

Mr. Thatcher said, "Business must be slacking off for T. Jay to buy that mummy."

It was a clear hint for Buzzer to tell what he knew.

Carrie was sure Father knew where Buzzer sold most of his newspapers, but he'd no more admit it than Buzzer would tell her what went on inside the saloons and dance halls. All she knew was what she had time and patience to pry out of Willie.

"He needs it for Saturday," said Buzzer. "They're holding cockfights behind the Silver Dollar. Won't be nobody on the Rough-n-Ready side of Main Street. Without something to show, T. Jay might as well close up."

"Still, that's a lot to pay for a corpse. He could have had those two Judge Herker hanged for nothing."

"Henry!" Mrs. Thatcher glared as she handed him a platter of gingerbread. "Not at the table, please."

Buzzer grabbed a piece of cake. "I wouldn't have sold the mummy. I'd have showed it myself. Got one of those wagons or a tent and charged ten cents a look. With the crowd in town on Fourth of July, I'd have made a fortune."

"And everybody could see it," said Carrie.

"Everybody with ten cents," corrected Buzzer.

Carrie pointed to the mess on Willie's plate. "You going to finish that?"

He looked up at her, his eyes wide and sad. "It wasn't the mummy."

Her bewilderment must have shown because Willie added without any prompting, "Apache Sam. He didn't go 'cause of the mummy."

"Carrie," warned Mrs. Thatcher.

Carrie took her stack of dirty dishes to the kitchen table and returned for more. Father was helping Buzzer figure the cost of buying a tent and showing the mummy.

Lonnie was complaining loudly, "I want to see. I want to see, too."

"You don't know what they're talking about," Carrie told him.

"I do, too. The mummy. I want to see the mummy."

"You can't."

"I want to."

"So do I, but I can't. It's in a smelly old saloon."

Mother said, "Honestly, Carrie, I don't understand you at times. Why would you want to see a thing like that?"

"Because I never have." Remembering something Portia had read from *Harper's Weekly*, she quoted, "It gives a well-rounded development to a young lady's education."

The article had been about painting with watercolors, but Carrie thought it suited this occasion better.

"More likely give you nightmares," said Mr. Thatcher. "More coffee, Mother?"

Mrs. Thatcher went to get the pot.

"I want to see the mummy." Lonnie hadn't stopped his chant, just raised the volume and recaptured their attention. He could go on for hours when he took a notion.

"You'll see it all right," Carrie warned him. "If you don't keep quiet, it'll come and get you with its face all moldy and a smell like rotten potatoes."

She couldn't do it the way Portia did, with lots of fancy words and all the actions, but it was good enough to shut Lonnie up and earn a shocked, "Carrie!" from her mother. Buzzer grinned.

When her parents went upstairs to change clothes for the meeting, Lonnie trailed along. Buzzer and Willie lingered at the table to snitch the last three pieces of cake. When they reached the back porch, Carrie was waiting.

"You forgot firewood," she told them, keeping her eyes on Buzzer.

He said, "We'll get it tomorrow."

She side-stepped, blocking him. "Tonight. Now. Or I tell Mother you took one of her clothesline props."

He'd either lost it or hadn't finished with it because he stood still to hear the rest. Carrie ticked each item off on her fingers.

"You'll also fill the kettle and put it on the stove, soak the cooler, fill the water jar and empty the garbage bucket and put it back under the sink." She had to be careful of details. Once she'd searched half the morning for the bucket. "And you'll do it all now, before you leave."

"And if Willie and me do all this, you won't tell Mother about us borrowing the clothesline pole."

"That's right."

"Or what time we come home tonight."

Carrie pretended to think about it. She didn't want to give in too easily. At last she said, "As long as you're home before Father and Mother."

"It's a deal. Come on, Willie."

Carrie was surprised Buzzer hadn't dickered longer, but she didn't waste time puzzling over it. She flew through the kitchen and dining room, left the parlor doors open for a quick escape, rescued the magazine, opened the drapes for light and discovered she'd forgotten to close the window. It let a breeze into the stuffy room. She sank cross-legged onto the carpet and read. She was gnawing her finger over a sword fight when she heard her parents on the stairs.

"Damnation!" She read as she turned, read as she pushed the magazine behind the drape, and was in the dining room, parlor doors shut behind her, when Mother stepped in from the kitchen.

"Lonnie's in bed," she told Carrie. "I don't think he'll give you any trouble. Here, I'll finish clearing. You start washing."

She laid her mitts and reticule on the sideboard and began collecting the dirty plates. Carrie took a stack into the kitchen and put them on the table there. She smelled cigar smoke from the sitting room where Father was reading the *Epithet*. She knew he'd opened the drapes and windows to disperse the smoke. The sun would have the sitting room hot as the kitchen. She and Portia wouldn't be comfortable till after sundown. She felt sorrier for her father, though, sitting in there in a vest and jacket.

She rolled up her sleeves and took out the dishpan. The boys had kept their part of the bargain. The kettle held hot water and when she slipped outside to check, the water jar was full and the cooler soaking wet. The garbage bucket had been emptied, but a small brown lizard had been added to surprise her.

She waited until her mother took the tablecloth outside to shake, then put the lizard on the window sill over the sink. The sun was still too hot for it. It ran down the inside wall and behind the cupboard. Carrie hoped it would find a way outside before her mother found it.

The sun slanted through the window, forcing Carrie to squint down at the dishpan. Sweat broke out on her forehead and ran down her face. When she turned to the table for another stack of dishes, she met a breeze from the dining room. She faced into it gratefully, wiped the runnels from her face with her shoulders and turned back to the dishpan, the sun and the hot water.

Mrs. Thatcher began drying, holding the wet dishes well out from her starched ruffled waist. Carrie quickly wiped clean one end of the kitchen table.

"Stack them here," she told her mother. "Portia will help put them away."

Mr. Thatcher called from the sitting room, "Mother, it's time we were leaving."

"I'm almost ready." Mrs. Thatcher brought her things from the dining room, peering out the windows as she smoothed on her lace mitts. "I wonder where the boys are. I don't like them wandering off when snakes and things are coming out."

"In this heat they won't be out till after sunset," Carrie told her. "It's early yet."

"All the same, you never can tell." She checked her hair and the tilt of her hat in the mirror behind the back door. "I saved some gingerbread for you and Portia. It's in the cupboard."

"Thank you." Carrie smiled at her.

The clock in the sitting room chimed seven.

Mr. Thatcher called, "Emma!"

Mrs. Thatcher kissed Carrie's cheek, said, "See the boys get in before dark and don't forget that Portia is company," and hurried down the hall. Carrie heard Father say, "The *Epithet*'s playing up that mummy like it's the eighth wonder," before the front door closed behind them.

She dried her hands on her apron and tiptoed down the hall, listening for Lonnie. There was no sound. She walked past the stairs and opened the parlor door. A breeze welcomed her. She'd forgotten to close the drapes as well as the window. She hesitated, then opened them wide.

Parlor and sitting room doors faced each other across the hall. The breeze would sweep through and cool the sitting room, especially after the sun went down. She'd just have to remember to close up the parlor before Mother came home. She propped the door open with the chunk of silver ore Father kept on the curio shelf. She paused to listen upstairs and heard a noise.

"Lonnie Thatcher," she yelled, "you get back in bed. I know where that monster bug is. You give me any trouble and I'll have him come back and pinch you good."

She heard running feet and a jump on a bed, but no crying or begging for attention. She took the magazine to the sitting room and settled on a mohair chair near a front window.

The hero won the sword fight, took three columns of print to re-rescue the heroine and galloped across France pursued by Evil Forces. They caught the boat to England and were safe at last. Carrie sighed and closed the magazine. The story was a lot like one of Portia's theatricals, but it had given Carrie a glimpse of Paris and Calais.

In her whole life she'd known only mining towns, two before this one. When the high-grade ore petered out, the company would sell the mine and move Father to a new one. Carrie could hardly remember the first town, but she knew Stringtown was the most civilized. Mrs. Dollingwood said the Grand Palace Hotel equaled many in San Francisco, but it wasn't Brussels carpets and fresh oysters that mattered to

Carrie. It was being in New York or San Francisco or sailing the English Channel. Carrie had never even crossed the Colorado. When something interesting and strange like the mummy did turn up, she wasn't allowed to see it.

She checked the Dollingwood house. There was no sign of Portia so she got the newspaper from the table. Hunting for news of the mummy she skimmed over paragraphs, taking time to read: "Three scientific professors in New York City have assayed Miss Eusapia Palladino and found her to be a one hundred per cent bona fide spiritist which comes as no surprise to the citizens of that city who have consulted the comely lady. It is said that Miss Palladino is an even more accomplished spiritist than the world-famous Fox sisters, the spirits summoned by her being of a more energetic nature, lifting tables and blowing trumpets as well as table rapping. Citizens from Philadelphia to San Francisco have renowned spiritists to consult, but so far this scientific phenomenon has eschewed our prospering city, the only spirits in evidence being the bottled variety. The Grand Palace Hotel has just received a shipment of fine wines. . . ."

Carrie skipped the advertising and a lengthy description of the new marching uniforms of the volunteer fire company. Then she found it, three times as long as any other item on the page, full of the mummy's scientific value and how it would be a fine addition to the Smithsonian Institution, but not one word about how it looked, where it was found or who it might be. For that, wrote Mr. Weatherberry, one must patronize the Rough-n-Ready Saturday afternoon.

"Hellfire," said Carrie.

Buzzer and Willie were sure to see the mummy. She could question them, but she was tired of getting things secondhand. Besides, her brothers were as apt to miss what was there as Portia was to add things that weren't. Carrie wanted to see for herself.

She wondered if she could get Portia fired up about the mummy. Between Mrs. Dollingwood's social clubs and Mr. Dollingwood's law practice, they influenced a lot of public opinion. They'd gotten the gallows moved off Main Street and into a fenced yard. If Portia insisted on seeing the mummy, her parents would try to arrange it. Maybe they'd start a movement for a Smithsonian Institution for the Territory. There must be lots of scientific things in Arizona.

But Portia would probably say mummies weren't ladylike. Carrie searched the newspaper. Yes, it definitely said Miss Palladino was a lady, and if a lady could talk to a ghost she should be able to look at a mummy. They were both the leftovers of dead people.

Before she could get her arguments thought out, a door banged. Portia left the house across the street, carrying her basket of night things. Carrie went to open the front door.

"I thought you were coming early," she called. "It's after eight o'clock."

"We had dinner at the Grand Palace. Mama said she couldn't face cooking dinner, not with two meetings today. Then Papa met Judge Herker and they talked and talked and then I had to go home and change clothes again." She talked herself through the door and past Carrie. "Oh, somebody's coming." She sounded disappointed.

Carrie told her, "No, I just opened the parlor door to let the breeze through. Here's the magazine."

She tucked it into the basket so Portia wouldn't forget it, then led the way to the kitchen.

"Wait until I tell you what I heard. You won't believe it!" Portia set her basket on the table. "Remember Miss Brewster?"

The water had turned cold and scummy. Carrie added hot from the kettle and soaped the dishcloth.

"Of course," she said. "Dr. Brewster's sister from Philadelphia."

"Well, Miss Brewster is talking to ghosts."

"WHAT?" Carrie turned to stare at her.

"Yes, yes!" Portia danced around the table. "I said you wouldn't believe me."

"Is her house haunted?" Carrie tried to imagine meeting a ghost at the foot of the stairs.

"I don't know about that. Mama forgot about me being in the room, but I still missed a lot. But I do know that Miss Brewster goes to a spiritist and they have a séance and the spirits come and talk to them and Mama says my Aunt Jennifer in San Francisco does, too. Oh, Carrie!" Portia did Pleading, clasping her hands. "Let's have a séance!"

4

The Spirit's Scare

"Isn't it ever going to get dark?" complained Portia.

Carrie, scrubbing the last greasy pot, didn't bother to answer. Portia draped the drying towel over her shoulder and carried a stack of clean plates to the cupboard.

"There's a lizard in here." She put a hand over her heart. "A lizard! I think I shall swoon!"

She staggered backward, groping behind her for the table. She found it and sank into the chair beside it, her head lolling over the high wooden back, her eyes closed. Carrie turned and watched.

When all movement stopped, she said, "There was a lizard used to sun himself on your porch railing every morning last autumn. You didn't swoon then. You said it was an enchanted prince."

Without opening her eyes Portia said, "Last autumn I was a silly child. Today I'm a sensitive young lady."

"And lizards make you swoon."

"Yes. How do I look?"

"Like somebody who fainted."

"I do?" The eyes opened and the head came forward so Portia could examine herself. She laid her head back and flapped the end of the dishtowel before her face. "I should have a lace handkerchief to waft."

"How can you waft it if you've fainted?"

"Swooned."

"What's the difference?"

"Swooning's more ladylike." Portia straightened. "Is it dark yet?"

"No." Carrie finished the pot, emptied the dishpan and wiped it. "If one little lizard makes you swoon, what are you going to do if we see a ghost?"

"We won't see it. We'll hear it." Portia carried the rest of the dishes to the cupboard. If the lizard was still there, she gave no sign. She stood beside Carrie and looked out the window. "It's going to take forever to get dark. I know what we can do! I have a new recipe."

Carrie hoped it wasn't the one for hair rinse. She'd

used all her threats to get Buzzer to do her chores. She hadn't any left over to get whiskey.

"It's a face mask," Portia explained. "Egg white and raw oatmeal. Mrs. Bender says it does wonders for the complexion."

There was plenty of oatmeal in the pantry, but Carrie didn't know what Mother would say about using eggs for a face mask. Before she could object, Portia said, "I'll go get some eggs. You get the oatmeal," and was gone down the hall and out the front door. Carrie barely had time to clean the kitchen before Portia was back with a bowl of egg whites.

Carrie brought out the oatmeal and watched it being mixed with the egg whites.

"You first," said Portia.

Carrie sat by the table and closed her eyes. The mixture was smoothed on, cool and not slimy as she'd expected.

"There." Portia giggled. "You look ghastly, like an ogre from the mines. My turn now."

She wiped her hands and took Carrie's place on the chair. Carrie spread the lumpy mixture over Portia's upturned face, working carefully around the eyes and mouth. She finished and took bowl and spoon to the sink.

Portia said, "How do I look?"

"Moldy."

Portia went to peer in the mirror behind the back door. "I do! Especially in this light." Her voice sank to a whisper. "Do you think it's time?"

"It's still light outside." Carrie rinsed the bowl and spoon and put them away.

"It's taking so long," wailed Portia.

"You're the one said we had to wait for dark."

"Of course. Did you ever hear of a ghost appearing in daylight?" She touched her cheeks with her fingertips. "It's pulling! Do you feel it?"

Carrie nodded. "How long do we leave it on?"

"Mrs. Bender didn't say. I guess the longer the better." She giggled. "I can hardly open my mouth."

Carrie put the dish and spoon away and went out to swamp the cooler. Portia helped her carry water and soak the burlap. When they were back inside, the kitchen seemed considerably darker. Carrie lit the lamp.

"It has to be dark," said Portia.

"One lamp isn't daylight." Even with the wick turned high, large corners of the room were in deep shadow. "Besides, you said the spirits didn't appear. They just blew trumpets and banged around."

"Table rapped," corrected Portia. "They rap on the table."

Carrie was getting the knack of talking without moving her lips, but Portia's *b*'s came out *d*'s.

"The boys are going to need a light." If a ghost did appear, Carrie wanted to see it. "I can leave it here and we can have the séance in the sitting room."

"I'll go see if it's dark enough."

While waiting for Portia's verdict, Carrie shut and

locked the back doors and the windows opening onto the back porch. She didn't want Buzzer catching them in the middle of the séance. She found Portia closing the drapes on the front sitting room windows.

"That makes it darker," she explained.

It also hid them from nosy people in the street. The side window still let in the fading light and drew the breeze from the parlor. Carrie locked the front door and listened upstairs for Lonnie. He must have fallen asleep.

"All ready," she told Portia. "What do we do?"

"We sit at a table." She moved chairs to the small bentwood table. "I think we'd better take everything off."

Books, carved box, china figures, newspaper, sewing basket and fringed cloth were quickly moved onto chair seats, easily found in the dimness. Carrie sat at the table facing the kitchen door. Portia settled opposite, a dark shape against the lamplight.

Forcing herself not to whisper, Carrie said, "What now?"

"We hold hands." She reached across the table and took Carrie's. "Now one of us calls the spirits."

"You call."

Portia knew dozens of recitations. There must be something in them she could use. They sat until dimness became dark. Even sound faded. Birds hushed. Insects were still. Only the breeze remained, lightly moving Carrie's hair.

Carrie whispered, "Go ahead."

Portia whispered back, "I'm thinking."

Carrie shivered. This was as exciting as the time she'd made Buzzer and Willie take her with them to steal food offerings from a new grave in the Chinese cemetery. They'd met no ghosts, though. Not even a guard or a late mourner. She had higher hopes for tonight, spiritism being a scientific phenomenon that even Miss Brewster practiced.

"All right," whispered Portia. "I'm ready. Now don't let go of my hands. No matter what happens. We mustn't break the circle."

Their clasped hands made an oblong, not a circle, but Carrie let it pass.

In her recitation voice Portia began, "Is there a spirit here before me, a table ready for its hand? Speak, oh speak, dread spirit, if you can. Knock once for yea, twice for nay. Speak! Do you attend me?"

She paused. There was no sound. Even the breeze had stopped.

"Speak, oh spirit! Speak to us and in peace depart. Knock once for yes, twice for no. Are you here?" Portia gasped. Her hands gripped Carrie's painfully as she whispered, "There's something here. It brushed my skirt. Do you feel it?"

Grimacing at the pull of the face mask, Carrie turned her head as far to each side as she could. The lamplight from the kitchen seemed to hinder her vision rather than help. She could make out no unfamiliar shadow, no shape that should not be there. She wished Portia hadn't closed the front drapes.

"Spirit," called Carrie, "speak up!"

Portia squeezed her hands for silence and took up the call. "Spirit, answer me. Rap once for yea, twice for nay. Answer, spirit, I beseech you. I know you walk this mortal coil. I feel your presence. Speak to me."

Silence.

Talking to the spirit as she would her brothers, Carrie said aloud, "You're scared!"

The knock shook the table.

Portia screamed.

Carrie jerked her hands free and ran to the kitchen for the lamp.

"Don't leave me," yelped Portia.

She trailed Carrie as she checked the doors and windows, then hurried upstairs. The bedrooms were empty except for Lonnie. He was curled up asleep.

"I never heard of a scared ghost," Carrie whispered. Her voice was husky and her hands shook so that the coal oil sloshed dangerously in the lamp base. She was glad to get downstairs and put it back on the kitchen table.

Portia's eyes were shining. She hugged herself.

"I did it. I really did it! I'm a spiritist." She started to grin and winced. She scratched at the dried face mask. "Maybe this is what scared him."

"Why should it?"

"It looks beastly and moldy. It reminds him of the grave. Let's take it off and try again."

While they were filling the basin, fists pounded on the back door.

"Hey, let us in," yelled Buzzer. "What you got the door locked for?"

Then he and Willie were peering in the window, pointing and laughing. Buzzer called, "What you two got up for? It's Fourth of July, not Halloween."

Portia bent over the basin, scrubbing furiously. Carrie yanked open the door and let them in. Buzzer grinned up at her and said, "Where you been keeping that face? It's an improvement on the one you've been using."

Through clenched teeth Carrie said, "I thought you were coming home late."

"I am. Just now I need something." Buzzer opened the door to the pantry under the stairs. "Bring that lamp over here, Willie."

Willie did, all the time looking up at Carrie and grinning. That unnerved her more than anything Buzzer could say. She envied Portia her clean face.

Buzzer set out half a dozen large canning jars and signaled Willie to put the lamp back.

Carrie said, "Does Mother know you're taking those?"

Buzzer laughed. "You don't see me and I don't see you and gorgeous Portia over there."

Stalemate, Carrie decided. "You better get back here before Father and Mother."

"Don't worry. Me and Willie keep our faces clean."

Hooting with laughter, he and Willie picked up the jars and left. They tapped a farewell on the window as they crossed the porch.

Portia sniffed. "I'm glad I don't have any brothers."

Carrie wished she didn't either, but it seemed disloyal to say it. She washed her face and they tried again to summon the spirit, without success. They put the sitting room in order and went back to the kitchen table. While they ate their gingerbread, Carrie wrote on white wrapping paper from the Bon Ton everything they could remember of what Portia had said the first time.

Portia moistened her fingertip and dabbed at the crumbs on the plate. "It must have been your brothers. They broke the spell. Spells are very delicate things."

Carrie wondered if she was right. Not about the spell, but about the boys. When she'd checked the doors and windows, she'd forgotten the water barrel under the parlor window. Could the boys have crawled in, knocked on the table and crawled out again? They'd been at the door right afterward and surely the face mask hadn't been all that funny, especially to Willie.

Portia was guessing at the identity of the spirit. "It can't be someone haunting your house. Nobody's died here yet."

"Maybe an Indian. Or the mummy."

Portia hadn't heard about the mummy. Her eyes brightened as she listened.

Carrie told her, "I'll get the newspaper and you can read about it."

She didn't take a lamp into the sitting room. She pulled a chair up to the bentwood table and sat where she'd been when the knock sounded. Neither Buzzer nor Willie could have knocked on the table without crawling into the room, and nobody could have entered the room without Carrie seeing him. Nobody.

She whispered the word, separating the syllables and giving it added meaning. The parlor door looked like the entrance to a tomb.

"Just a scared nobody," she whispered, but it didn't help.

She grabbed the *Epithet* and rushed to the kitchen. Even if she did catch holy Hannah, she wasn't going to close up the parlor until Mother came home to keep her company.

5

Portia's Grand Swoon

Carrie bit off a length of thread and glanced down the street before trying to thread the needle. She was lengthening the sleeves and skirt of her Sunday dress. She'd brought it to the Dollingwood front porch on the excuse it was cooler, but she and Portia were really waiting for the newspaper. Buzzer didn't bring Father's copy until he'd finished his sales on Main Street. The Dollingwoods took the *Epithet* from a news carrier and received it in the early afternoon.

Portia lolled in the swing, one foot tucked under

her, the other pushing against the porch floor. With an especially hard push, she declared, "Emma Lou Smedley gives me the heaves."

"You shouldn't lay down while you swing," Carrie told her.

"I mean last night. She couldn't open her mouth without reminding us she was riding on the Shakespeare Society's float." She exaggerated a Southern accent. "Number six! I declare, that's the number of horses going to pull little old me on the float on the Fourth of July." In her own voice she added, "It's a wonder I wasn't sick all over her lotto cards."

"It might have been better than telling about our séance."

"Why?" Portia turned to look at her. "Our séance was a good deal more interesting than Emma Lou Smedley's old float. How can you sew in this heat?"

Carrie had a linen towel over her knees. She wiped her palm on it and started hemming the second sleeve.

"You should have waited till we tried again," Carrie told her. "We only had that one knock for an answer."

"Because the spirit was frightened, which proves it was the mummy." Portia sat up to give room to her sweeping gestures. "The mummy is an Indian, a chief far from his tribe, lost among the Apache."

Carrie gave her full attention to Portia's story.

"He was the handsome, gallant Chickalimmy, chief of the Chickamaugas."

"Chickamauga was a battle in the War," Carrie reminded her.

"Doubtless named after the chief's tribe."

"But it's way back East. How did a Chickamauga get out here?"

Portia dropped her voice. "Vengeance, that's why he came. His beautiful bride was stolen, the Princess Minnitonka. Chief Chickalimmy vowed revenge. He trailed them over the mountains. He trailed them over the rivers." Portia stood to pantomime the warrior's search. "To the far Mississippi he trailed them."

Carrie interrupted. "Trailed who?"

"The Apaches who'd stolen his bride. Geronimo. No, the *Epithet* says the mummy is ancient." She paused, then said, "Chickalimmy trailed Mucho Gusto, ancient chief of the dread Apache. Where was I?"

"At the Mississippi River."

"Yes. Oh, here he comes!"

She brushed past Carrie, down the steps, and ran to meet the newsboy. She ran awkwardly, knees together and feet kicking sideways. Carrie supposed it was ladylike, but it didn't cover ground very fast. She'd finished hemming the sleeve before Portia was back with the *Epithet*.

She pulled out the inside pages and handed them to Carrie. There was silence as their fingers ran down the columns of tiny crooked type.

"You must have gotten the good part," said Portia.

"This is all about General Crook not catching Geronimo."

Carrie grinned and pretended to read. "There's a shipment of hats at the Bon Ton, straight from New York and faithfully copied from Paris fashions."

"Let's go see them. Can you go this afternoon?"

Carrie was sorry she'd teased her. "After we finish the newspaper."

There was another silence, broken by pained sighs from Portia. Suddenly she cried, "Here it is! Listen. 'Last evening Miss Emma Lou Smedley entertained friends at her parents' residence on Third Street. Part of the evening was given to making rosettes for marchers in the Fourth of July parade. Miss Smedley will grace the Stringtown Shakespeare Society's float in that forthcoming event. Miss Smedley will be remembered as a member of the cast in the Society's performance of *Never Forget*.'"

Portia looked up from the newspaper. "Then how did they forget me? I had just as big a part as Emma Lou Smedley."

"Neither of you had a part," Carrie reminded her. "You just sat around the stage like part of the scenery."

"But I was on stage as long as she was."

"But you're never here on the Fourth of July."

"And I won't be this year if they hurry up and catch Geronimo. Oh, Carrie, if I have to stand on Main Street and watch Emma Lou gloat over me, I'll die!" She was quiet a moment, then said, "I'll swoon. That's what I'll do, just as the float passes."

"You better be sure there's somebody to catch you."

"When a lady swoons, there is always a gentleman to catch her."

"Then I should think the gentleman would be somewhat suspicious."

Portia looked genuinely surprised. "Whatever for?"

Carrie prodded her back to important subjects. "Is there any more in the *Epithet*?"

Portia found the place and read, " 'The balance of the evening was devoted to a hilarious game of lotto, and the guests thanked their charming hostess for a delightful evening that was also of benefit to our community. The Ladies' Aide of the. . . .' That's all. Not one word about the séance."

Carrie was relieved.

Portia looked ready to cry. "Emma Lou never told Mr. Weatherberry, that's why. But those girls were all goggle-eyed last night. Somebody must have told someone."

"I think Emma Lou did." Carrie nodded at two women strolling down Third Street. "Isn't that Mrs. Smedley?"

"And Judge Herker's wife. They must be coming to call on Mama."

Carrie folded her dress and gathered her sewing things.

Portia said, "Remember those new hats at the Bon Ton? Let's ask quick if we can go see them."

Carrie dashed down the steps. "Meet me at my house."

"Immediately!" Portia disappeared through her front door.

Carrie found her mother in the sitting room, lengthening Lonnie's short pants. The room smelled of being closed all day.

"Can I go downtown with Portia?" Carrie asked. "She wants to look at some new hats at the Bon Ton."

Mrs. Thatcher patted her face and neck with a handkerchief and nodded. "Stop at the Emporium and get me some dark blue thread. Have them put it on the account and get a nickel's worth of candy for yourself."

"Thank you." Carrie strained toward the hall door.

"Tidy up and put on the pink calico before you go."

"I will."

Carrie dashed upstairs, threw the things she'd been carrying on her bed and pulled off her dress. She poured water from the pitcher into the basin and splashed her face and hands. She left her braids alone but smoothed the front hair and patted on water to hold it down until she got past Mother. She ran downstairs and stood to let her mother hook up her dress.

"Don't forget the blue thread," said Mrs. Thatcher. "And watch where you step."

Carrie heard footsteps on the front porch and hurried outside. Portia hadn't changed clothes but she still looked more dressed up than Carrie. She had brushed out her braids and tied her long hair with a lavender ribbon. She wore white lace mitts and carried an unopened white parasol edged with lavender.

"Shall we go?" she asked in a very grown-up way, then turned and ran as fast as she could.

Carrie quickly outdistanced her and waited at the corner. "It's too hot to run."

"I know." Portia was panting. She opened the parasol. "I wanted to get away before Mrs. Smedley got around to telling about our séance."

"You can't be sure that's what they came for." Carrie walked slowly, sharing the parasol and giving Portia time to catch her breath.

"I'm sure. What I don't know is what Mama and Papa are going to think about it."

"You should have thought of that last night."

"I know."

"And you didn't have to be so dramatic telling it."

Portia sighed. "I know, but it was such fun. Did you see Henrietta Moyer's face?"

"And Hester upset the lotto cards."

They giggled and clung to each other, comparing memories of the night before. When they reached the boardwalk on Main Street, they sobered and walked more primly.

"I have to stop at the Emporium," Carrie said. "Where shall we go first?"

"The Bon Ton," Portia decided. She was using her ladylike voice. "I do dislike carrying purchases."

Parasol at the proper angle, she started across Main Street, picking her way around horse droppings without a noticeable glance. Carrie had to give crossing her full attention to reach the opposite boardwalk with clean shoes.

They strolled in the shade, stopping at every window. Wagons stood along the walk, and ranch women and miners' wives, doing their Saturday shopping and visiting, passed the girls.

They were inspecting three pairs of high-button shoes and a beaded purse that had been in the Mercantile window since March when Portia said, "Where are the boys?"

Carrie stared at her.

"The boys. There aren't any boys around."

There were, but they were all Lonnie's age or younger. No men, young or old, lounged against the storefronts, nor was Willie standing lookout in front of the Rough-n-Ready. Carrie squinted across the street. Her eye was caught by the Silver Dollar sign and she remembered what Buzzer had said about the cockfights.

"They're all over behind the Silver Dollar," she told Portia, "watching roosters kill each other."

Portia wrinkled her nose. "How disgusting." But she didn't sound as if she cared.

As they lingered at one window after another Carrie wondered if the mummy was drawing any business to the Rough-n-Ready. Nothing came from the saloons they passed but the smell of beer. No noise, no laughter, no piano. Dinkum's had a penciled sign on the door: *Gone to the Fights.*

"Portia," Carrie said suddenly, "how would you like to see the mummy?"

"Not especially."

"But you want to talk to it."

"That's different. Good afternoon, Mrs. Bradley."

While Portia reported to Mrs. Bradley on the state of her parents' health and how she liked the heat, Carrie organized the kind of arguments that would work with Portia.

As soon as Mrs. Bradley moved on, Carrie said, "I don't think that mummy's ever going to talk to you again, not if you won't pay a simple courteous call when you're right in the neighborhood."

"Carrie Thatcher, nice girls don't even look at a saloon let alone go inside one."

"A lady always returns a call. Besides, what if the saloon is empty? What if nobody will know? We can go around back to the delivery entrance. Nobody will see us."

"No!" Portia walked briskly past Murchison's Feed and Hardgoods, headed for the Bon Ton.

"If that mummy talked to us, stands to reason he'll want to see us, too." They were passing the Rough-n-

Ready. Carrie took Portia's arm and slowed her. "Listen."

Only silence and saloon smell came from behind the half doors.

"No," said Portia.

Carrie wanted to jump and scream in frustration. Here was a golden opportunity and she was missing it. Desperately she offered, "All right, you stay here on lookout while I go inside."

Portia stared at her, mouth open.

"Please," Carrie started to beg, then looked past her and muttered, "Oh-oh."

Henrietta Moyer and Emma Lou Smedley were walking toward them, arm in arm. Portia groaned and stepped to one of the Bon Ton's narrow windows, trying to hide between it and her parasol. From the way Emma Lou raised her voice and began talking about the Fourth of July parade, it was clear Portia had been seen, though the girls ignored her as they swept into the Bon Ton.

As they passed Portia and Carrie, Emma Lou drawled, "Mama says I can put my hair up when I ride on the float. It'll be ever so much cooler, don't you think, Henrietta?"

Portia turned her back on the window and muttered, "I hope she falls off the float and breaks her goosey neck."

Emma Lou seemed to have found a way to get Portia's attention—ignore her. Carrie took a deep breath and walked on, past the entrance to the Bon Ton and its other window. She was turning into the alley when Portia caught her sleeve and asked, "Where are you going?"

Calm as she could, Carrie said, "To see the mummy."

"Carrie Thatcher!"

"You don't have to come. Just stand out here and if Mr. Jay or anyone comes along, start talking to them in front of the Rough-n-Ready. Talk loud enough for me to hear and long enough for me to scoot out the back."

"But. . . ."

Carrie loosened Portia's hold on her sleeve, took a quick look both ways on Main Street and hurried between the Bon Ton and the Grand Palace. She wished she had Buzzer and Willie with her. Before she turned behind the Bon Ton, Portia caught up.

"I'm not standing out there for Emma Lou Smedley to see and make sport of," she declared. She folded her parasol, looked nervously at the little adobe houses backing onto the delivery alley and whispered, "Somebody will see us."

"Won't matter if they do. They're Chinese." Of course, one of Willie's friends might tell him. Carrie wished Portia had stood lookout the way Willie did for Buzzer. No, it was better to have company and someone to share the shame if they did get caught.

As if reading her thoughts, Portia said in her recitation voice, "This is a dread and fearsome enterprise. Lead on!"

"Shh!" This was no time for Portia to get carried away. Sometimes she had less sense than Lonnie. Carrie took Portia's hand and led her to the back door of the Rough-n-Ready. She listened, then tugged Portia into the dark and cool. They stood hand in hand, waiting for their eyes to adjust, then crept past kegs and crates to a doorway.

They stepped into one end of the saloon, next to a narrow stair. The bar was to their right, against the back wall. Facing them was the street wall, the half doors in the center. It was a strange view of Main Street, just skirt bottoms, parasols and hats.

"Carrie!" Portia pulled back toward the storage room.

Carrie whispered, "We're here. We might as well see."

Some of the wooden tables held cards, dice and faro boxes. Chairs were tilted against them, four or six to a table. There were enough hanging lamps for half a dozen houses, but in spite of them the saloon looked drab and dirty, not at all what Carrie had expected. She dragged Portia around the end of the bar, ignoring her whispered protests.

On the back wall hung a painting, larger than life size, of a naked woman on a red velvet couch. Willie had never told her about that. Beneath the painting were cabinets filled with glasses and mugs. On top of the cabinets, propped on black velvet, was a shriveled form, knees pulled up to its chest.

"There it is," said Carrie.

Portia hushed her, but Carrie scarcely heard. The mummy was as naked as the woman in the painting, but smaller than life size, and looked older than the mountains. The eyelids had sunk into the sockets. Hair clung to the scalp. It was dead but it was still here and looked as if it wanted to live. It made Carrie sad in a way she'd never felt before.

It's grief, she decided, grief and mourning. But she didn't know if she mourned for all the things the mummy had missed or for the ones that she would never know. She turned to Portia, ready to leave.

But Portia stepped past her to the bar, pulling hard on her hand. "Hold me, Carrie! It's calling. Don't you hear?"

Carrie heard a man's voice bellow, "What the devil are you two doing in here?"

She hauled Portia toward the back door, but Portia kept resisting, her free arm outstretched to the mummy behind the bar.

"It's calling," she cried. "Don't you hear? It wants ...it...."

She pulled her hand from Carrie's, staggered backward three steps and fell.

6

The Mummy's Move

Before Portia hit the floor, Mr. Jay ran from the stairs and caught her. He shifted the limp form to one arm so he could take the cigar from his mouth. He pointed it at Portia and asked Carrie, "Is this Ben Dollingwood's girl?"

Too scared to speak, Carrie nodded.

T. Jay muttered something about being scalped, then told Carrie, "Doc Brewster's over behind the Silver Dollar. You better fetch him."

Carrie found her voice. "Don't you have a hand-kerchief or something?"

"Handkerchief?" he bellowed.

"To waft."

"No, and I don't have any smelling salts. And if I did have, I wouldn't keep her in here to use them. I'm taking her over to the Grand Palace. You go get Doc Brewster."

He started to lift Portia, noticed the cigar in his hand and thrust it at Carrie. "Hold this."

Carrie took it. Mr. Jay lifted Portia and maneuvered her feet first through the swinging doors. Her face hung upside down. Carrie watched the eyes and mouth for a signal but there was no sign of consciousness.

She picked up the parasol, tried to dust it off against her skirt and pushed her shoulder against the doors. She stepped from the saloon onto Main Street, the parasol in one hand and Mr. Jay's lighted cigar in the other, and came face to face with Mrs. Kelly.

"Carrie Thatcher," she demanded, "does your mother know what you're doing?"

Women who'd been watching Mr. Jay and his burden turned to stare at Carrie.

She held up the cigar. "This is Mr. Jay's. I'm just holding it for him."

"Get rid of it," ordered Mrs. Kelly, but didn't step aside so Carrie could toss it into the street. "What were you doing in there? What's wrong with the Dollingwood girl?"

"It was the mummy. Excuse me." She tried to sidle past Mrs. Kelly but the woman blocked her way.

"What do you mean? The mummy did something to her?"

"Excuse me. I have to get Doc Brewster." Carrie gestured with the cigar.

Mrs. Kelly drew back. Carrie ran past her, jumped off the walk and ran across the street. She didn't have time to watch her feet, but it looked as if Mother would have more than dirty shoes to scold about. When she reached the sunny side, Carrie dropped the cigar and glanced around.

Across the street, Mr. Jay was carrying Portia into the Grand Palace. A group of women led by Mrs. Kelly swept after them and everyone on both sides of Main Street gawked at the procession. Carrie ducked between Moyer's Pharmacy and the Last Chance Saloon and came out behind them.

These buildings backed onto a steep hillside. Behind the Silver Dollar a cock pit had been dug into the hill and half the men and boys were gathered around it. The rest were crowded at the tables set out behind the Silver Dollar as a bar. The Last Chance and some of the other saloons had set out makeshift bars too, but the business was mostly at the Silver Dollar's.

Carrie slowed to a shuffle. She'd never seen so many men in one lump before with no women on their arms to put her at ease. One or two noticed her and nudged their neighbors. Soon most had turned to stare. She felt as if she's been shoved on stage in the middle of one of Portia's theatricals. She stood twisting the parasol and trying to remember her lines.

"Carrie." Willie pulled at her arm, turning her around. "You oughtn't to be here."

"I have to get Doc Brewster. Something's happened to Portia."

"I'll get the Doc. You just go away."

Now it was Carrie who held onto Willie. "T. Jay took her to the Grand Palace. Send Doc Brewster over there."

If Willie wondered how T. Jay had gotten involved with Portia Dollingwood, he didn't ask. He just looked up at Carrie with solemn eyes.

She found herself stammering, "The mummy did something, I think. A spell or something. She couldn't help it."

Willie scooted off. Two Mexicans uncovered large bird cages and stepped into the pit. Men moved closer to it. Again Carrie was conscious of stares and groups of men discussing her. Two walked purposely toward her. She turned on her heel and went back between the buildings. Angry tears stung her eyes.

She had a perfectly good reason to be in their old alley. And she was the same Carrie Thatcher who'd walked down Main Street ten minutes before, so why did they frighten her and make her feel ashamed? It wasn't fair.

She didn't worry about getting back on Main Street

unseen. By supper time everybody in Stringtown would be talking about where she'd been. She forced her head up and marched across to the Grand Palace and into the lobby.

Portia reclined on the divan looking just as she did when playing the Lily Maid of Astolat. Half a dozen women hovered over her. Mrs. Kelly flapped a handkerchief before her face, but it wasn't lace nor was it wafted. Mrs. Kelly's energetic waves raised enough breeze to stir Mr. Jay's hair. He leaned over the back of the divan, watching.

"Where's the doctor?" he asked Carrie.

"Where's the smelling salts?" asked Mrs. Kelly. "She needs smelling salts."

"It's coming." Mr. Reeter, manager of the Grand Palace, hovered nervously around the group. "Would you ladies like some tea?"

Mrs. Kelly glared at him. "Certainly not! Not at a time like this."

T. Jay took a cigar from his inside coat pocket. "Do you ladies mind if I smoke?"

"We certainly do," said Mrs. Kelly.

They glared at each other, but Mr. Jay returned the cigar. Carrie wondered if he'd been waiting for the one she'd been holding.

"Ah, here's Dr. Brewster." Mr. Reeter rushed to escort the doctor across the blue Brussels carpet to the divan.

"Didn't you have any smelling salts?" said the doctor.

"Coming!" Mr. Reeter scurried off.

"If smelling salts will help," said Mrs. Kelly, still looking at Mr. Jay. "This may be something far more serious."

Mr. Jay leaned over the divan. "Just what are you implying, Mrs. Kelly?"

"I'm implying that mummy, Mr. T. Jay." She leaned forward so they were almost nose to nose over Portia. "That mummy is inhuman. Get rid of it."

Carrie wished Portia could see Mr. Jay. He did Dramatic Poses using only his face. It went from Dread to Relief to Amusement to Anger.

"Mrs. Kelly," he said, "you are loony with the heat. Doc, you better examine *her*."

"I'd better examine somebody pretty quick," said the doctor. "I'm missing the first match."

"Oh, the poor child." Mrs. Kelly drew back so the doctor could get to Portia.

He took her pulse, then lifted her eyelids one at a time. "What happened?"

Mrs. Kelly and the ladies looked at Carrie, who gnawed the handle of the parasol. Surely if Portia was play-acting she'd have made some sign by now. When Dr. Brewster lifted her eyelids, her eyes stared into nothing. It was frightening.

"Well?" said Dr. Brewster.

Carrie had nothing to go by but Portia's confusing words and actions. "The mummy seemed to be pulling her. She said she could hear it calling."

"I knew it," said Mrs. Kelly. "It had to be some

heathen spell. Why else would a nice girl enter a den of wickedness like the Rough-n-Ready?"

She glared at Mr. Jay who glared at Carrie and demanded, "Why didn't you stop her?"

"It happened so fast and she pulled so hard. . . ."

"Where's my daughter?" Mr. Dollingwood strode across the lobby. He nudged the doctor aside, knelt by Portia and took her hands in his. "Portia, little one."

Her eyelids fluttered. Her breast rose and fell with deep breaths. She murmured, "Alahashy."

Mrs. Kelly signaled for silence, though no one had tried to speak.

"Mishagoola . . . Chickamauga!" There were two more heaving breaths, then her eyes opened. She stared at the faces around her and said, "Where am I?"

"Praise God," said Mrs. Kelly. "She's recovered her senses."

"If she ever lost them," said Dr. Brewster.

Portia's father stood to face him. "What do you mean by that, Dan?"

Several women had joined Mrs. Kelly's group. Dr. Brewster looked at the watching faces and said, "I'll discuss it with you later. I've no time this afternoon."

"He called me." Portia's voice was faint but very clear. It gained strength as she went on. "He called and no one but I could hear. It was so sad." She clasped her hands prayerfully under her chin. "I had to answer even if it meant venturing into that place."

Mrs. Kelly patted her hand. The ladies murmured. Portia shuddered lightly and turned her face to the divan's back. Dr. Brewster muttered something about his sister and picked up his bag.

"Wait," said Mr. Dollingwood. "What care should she have?"

"Keep her home for a while." He started for the door.

"You mean rest and quiet?"

But the doctor was gone. T. Jay hurried after him, stopping to light a cigar before he stepped outside.

"Scientific men are so impatient," said one of the ladies.

"But Dr. Brewster's a good man," said another.

"No churchgoer, though," said Mrs. Kelly. "And heaven knows there are enough churches in String-town now that he could find one to suit him."

Portia called weakly, "Carrie. Where's Carrie?"

"She's right here," said Mr. Dollingwood.

Portia raised her head and gestured toward Carrie. "Dear Carrie. She tried to halt me but it was too late. The power was too strong. She tried to stop me but everything went black."

"Poor dear," said Mrs. Kelly.

Mr. Reeter rushed up with a small blue bottle. "Here it is, the smelling salts."

Mrs. Kelly waved him away. "We'll have tea in-stead. You'd like tea, dear, wouldn't you? It would do you good. And have some chairs brought, Mr. Reeter."

"Immediately." He rushed off again.

"Carrie." Mr. Dollingwood motioned her to him. "I'm going to the livery stable to hire a buggy. Will you stay with Portia and ride home with us?"

"Yes, sir!"

"Thank you." He assured Portia he'd be right back, bowed to the ladies and left.

Mexicans in blue and white uniforms brought chairs and a small table to the divan. Mr. Reeter handed out palmetto fans and the ladies settled themselves to discuss events. Portia sighed and closed her eyes, clearly unable to converse. That left Carrie to answer questions and she still wasn't sure what had happened.

"Excuse me," she said, mostly to Mrs. Kelly. "I must watch for Mr. Dollingwood's return."

On her way across the lobby Carrie noticed two figures sitting cross-legged behind a potted palm. She stopped to ask, "How long have you been here?"

Buzzer grinned. "Long enough."

Willie looked worried for her.

They got up and followed her to the door. She stayed inside where she wouldn't be noticed by passers-by. As her brothers went out to Main Street, Buzzer told her something she already knew. "Are you going to catch it tonight!"

Carrie tried not to think about it. She tapped

Portia's parasol against her leg as if impatiently waiting for someone. Two ladies came to see Portia, voices hushed as if at a funeral. Frank Ainsley rolled by on the sprinkler. Tea was served.

Carrie was doubly glad to have escaped the ladies' circle. She couldn't have brought herself to "accidentally" spill the tea on the carpet nor could she have drunk it, not in the suffocating heat of the lobby. The ladies poured and sipped as if it were winter. Maybe all that tight corseting kept their minds off the heat. Carrie sighed.

She'd never be a lady. Maybe she could run off and live with the Indians the way she and Essie had planned. They were going to wear long loose dresses with nothing underneath and cook meat on sticks so there'd be no potatoes to peel or pots to wash. And no cooler to swamp.

Now Essie had the chance, but Mother seemed to think she was keeping house just like everybody else. Maybe Essie just didn't want to scandalize Mother by telling about it. Carrie wished she had the postage to write her sister a private letter and ask.

Mr. Dollingwood stopped a surrey in front of the hotel, fastened the reins and climbed down. He seemed pleased to find Carrie waiting at the door.

"If you get in first," he said, "you can help me lift Portia."

Carrie nodded, too excited to trust her voice. Mr. Dollingwood handed her up just as he would have

Mrs. Dollingwood. Carrie perched on the back seat and felt quite elegant and regal. She was so intrigued with her elevated view of Main Street that she didn't notice Frank Ainsley and her brothers until Mr. Dollingwood carried Portia from the Grand Palace.

Frank Ainsley tipped his hat. "A fearsome experience, Miss Portia."

Portia smiled wanly. "Why, thank you, Mr. Ainsley."

That sounded peculiar to Carrie but nobody else seemed to notice. Buzzer looked smirky, but he often did.

"Can I be of assistance?" Frank Ainsley asked Mr. Dollingwood.

But Carrie had already taken Portia's arms and helped raise her into the high surrey. When they'd arranged themselves on the cracked leather seat, Carrie opened the parasol and held it between them.

Mrs. Kelly and the ladies had come out to watch and were blocking the traffic on the walk. Portia thanked Mrs. Kelly for her kindness. Mr. Dollingwood did also, then climbed into the front of the surrey and shook the reins. Frank Ainsley bowed. Willie smiled and waved. Carrie turned to wave back and saw Frank Ainsley talking with Mrs. Kelly.

Portia smiled at Carrie. Her eyes sparkled but she placed her finger over her lips. Carrie was happy not to talk. She didn't want to miss a second of the ride.

People she knew waved. Some she didn't know

smiled. Emma Lou and Henrietta stared open-mouthed. Carrie copied Portia's small gesture of return greeting. How grand it would be to ride down New York's Broadway or Market Street in San Francisco and have everyone on the sidewalk look and wave, even people you didn't know.

Then they turned down Third Street and there was no one on the sunny porches on Carrie's side, no one to greet until Lonnie came running around the Thatcher house to yell, "What's the matter, Carrie? Did you hurt your leg?"

"You stay right there," she yelled back and was furious with him for making her shout. She didn't need Portia to tell her that ladies didn't yell from grand carriages. Ladies didn't yell at all.

Mrs. Dollingwood came down the steps and path to ask her husband questions in a quiet, private voice. She heard only that Portia had fainted before she had her daughter out of the surrey and started toward the house. Carrie didn't wait for Mr. Dollingwood's hand. She jumped down and ran to give the parasol to Portia's mother.

"It's soiled," said Portia. "I'm sorry. I dropped it when I swooned."

Her mother made reassuring sounds and urged her toward the porch.

"May Carrie come in now?" asked Portia.

"Not now, dear." Mrs. Dollingwood smiled at Carrie. "Maybe tomorrow after church."

"But she's coming for dinner," Portia said. "You and Papa are going out for dinner. Remember?"

Carrie had forgotten. She was glad Portia hadn't. Maybe facing Mother and Father could be postponed.

Mrs. Dollingwood said, "We'll have to see about tonight."

Carrie's heart sank, but Portia smiled back at her and gave the little nod that meant she knew she could persuade her mother. Carrie was relieved. Partly because she wanted a good talk with Portia but mostly because she wanted to be away from home when her parents learned about today.

After being thanked by Mr. Dollingwood, Carrie crossed the street to where Lonnie jiggled and hopped. She told him, "You stop yelling at ladies, especially when they're in carriages."

"Where'd you go, Carrie?" he chanted. "Where'd you go?"

To pay him back for spoiling her grand and regal feeling, she told him, "To see the mummy," and was immediately sorry. He'd go screaming to Mother and Carrie'd have some tall explaining to do. But Lonnie was watching Mr. Dollingwood turn the surrey and didn't seem to hear.

Carrie let herself in the front hall. As she crept upstairs she heard her mother and Estrella in the kitchen. So far everything was quiet and normal. She went first to the boys' room and looked at the Penny Dreadfuls Buzzer hid under the mattress. He must be

saving all his pennies for fireworks for there were no
new lurid adventure stories. She was too worried to
read anyhow.

On her way back to her room she heard Lonnie
downstairs. "But she told me!"

Carrie leaned over the banister. From the kitchen
came her mother's, "She was only teasing. Estrella,
we'll have fried potatoes tonight and a hot dressing
on the greens."

Carrie clapped a hand over her mouth, stifling her
laughter. Lonnie had told and Mother hadn't believed
it. She hadn't believed her daughter would enter a
place like the Rough-n-Ready. Would she believe
Buzzer? Not that it mattered. Father would hear of it
on his way home or Mrs. Kelly would come calling.
It was just a matter of time. Carrie threw herself
across the bed.

"Hellfire!" If she were a boy she could run away
from home. Lots of boys younger than she were on
their own, but what could she do except become a
dance-hall or saloon girl and she wasn't desperate
enough for that. Not yet. She sighed heavily and half
wished Father would come home early so they could
get it over with.

As if in answer, there was a knock at the front
door.

7

"What's This I Hear?"

Carrie went softly to the head of the stairs. Her mother rustled and stepped along the hall.

Lonnie galloped after her. "Giddy-up, giddy-up!"

Mrs. Thatcher shushed him and opened the door. Mrs. Dollingwood was there. Mrs. Thatcher invited her in. Mrs. Dollingwood politely refused. Carrie squirmed in an agony of suspense, part of which was eased immediately. She was still invited to dinner. Mrs. Dollingwood wanted to know if she could come now.

"She may be able to calm Portia," explained Mrs.

Dollingwood. "She's very fretful and Dr. Brewster said she must have rest and quiet."

"Is she ill?" Mrs. Thatcher's voice was concerned.

Carrie held her breath. The silence couldn't have been as long as it seemed because she was still holding it when Mrs. Dollingwood said, "Portia's feeling a bit faint."

Bless Mrs. Dollingwood, thought Carrie.

"It must be the heat," said Mrs. Thatcher. "After all, it's her first summer in Stringtown."

"I expect that's it." Mrs. Dollingwood again declined to come in, and added, "I'd appreciate it if Carrie came over soon. Portia is extremely restless."

Carrie could imagine it. She hugged herself and danced the few steps to her bedroom, remembering to step out of sight before her mother turned from closing the front door.

Mrs. Thatcher called up the stairs, "Carrie, you're invited early to Portia's. Why didn't you tell me she was ailing?"

Carrie waited the time it would have taken her to come from the bed, then stepped into the doorway. "Dr. Brewster didn't think it was much of anything."

A pause, then, "Did you get my blue thread?"

Carrie clapped a hand to her forehead. "I forgot!"

"I expect so, in all the excitement. Lonnie says you came home in a carriage."

Her mother's sudden understanding loosened Carrie's tongue. "Oh, it was grand! Like royalty. It's nothing at all like riding in a buckboard or a stage-coach."

"Yes. Well, enjoy things while you can." Mrs. Thatcher squinted up the stairs. "Is that pink calico still presentable?"

"It's fine." Afraid her mother had forgotten, Carrie prompted, "When shall I go?"

"Soon as you comb your hair, wash your face and find a clean handkerchief. Let me see you before you go." As she went back to the kitchen, she said, "If you bring your comb down here, I'll do your hair."

Carrie sighed. There'd be no getting away with a lick and a dab this time. Her mother treated the Dollingwoods like San Francisco nabobs. "We move in different circles," was the way she put it. To Carrie it meant a lot of silly fussing every time she was invited for a meal or overnight stay.

She went back to her room, pulling the cord ties from her braids as she walked. After a few quick brushes she splashed water on her face, grabbed the ties and rushed downstairs to the kitchen.

Lonnie stood at the kitchen table watching his mother frost a yellow cake. The top layer slid slowly off the bottom one. Frosting oozed from between them and slid down the sides, settling in spreading mounds at the base. Mrs. Thatcher straightened the top layer and, lips tightly pressed, scraped up the frosting and spread it again on top of the cake.

"How can a body cook a decent meal in this heat?"

Mrs. Thatcher dropped spoon and knife in the frosting bowl and inspected Carrie. "You'll have to clean your shoes."

"Oh, Mother!"

"You are not going to the Dollingwoods with dirty shoes. When are you going to learn to look where you put your feet? You walk around as if this country had never seen a horse or cow."

"Or pig. Remember Tom wrote about New York City keeping pigs in the streets to eat the garbage?"

Mother smiled. "You'd learn to step lively there."

"Maybe you'd better send me East, too."

Carrie was shocked at herself. Not for the words but at how much she meant them. She waited anxiously for her mother's reaction, but Mrs. Thatcher's attention had returned to the cake.

"It'll have to be two single layers and if anyone wants icing, he can spoon it off the plate," she said. "The sooner you get at those shoes, Carrie, the sooner you'll be gone."

Gone across the street. Or maybe downtown. But never even as far as Tucson, which wasn't much bigger than Stringtown but at least you could ride part way on the railroad. She wasn't supposed to want to go anywhere or do anything. She rummaged in the storage cupboard for rags and brush and stomped out to the porch.

Estrella sat on the top step peeling potatoes. She smiled and tossed a peeled potato into the pot so that water splashed her bare feet. Her skirt was no longer than Carrie's and her waist had short sleeves and a low neckline. Mother had been scandalized when Carrie suggested dressing like that. What was she going to be when she learned Carrie really had gone into the Rough-n-Ready?

Trying to ignore the tight knot in her stomach, she crossed the dirt yard to the mesquite tree and stole the top rail from Lonnie's corral. She took it back to the steps, sat beside Estrella and removed her shoes. She quickly scraped soles and heels with the stick, then washed and buffed the leather portions with the rags. If she had slippers like Estrella wore on Sundays, she'd be finished. But she didn't and she wasn't. She grabbed the brush and attacked the cloth uppers.

"Too much," Estrella told her. "You'll make holes."

She tossed another potato, splashing Carrie's stockings. If they spotted, Mother would order them changed. Carrie pushed her feet into the shoes and clopped inside to find a buttonhook.

She prayed none of the buttons would pop. None did, and if her stockings had spots, Mother didn't notice. Lonnie had licked the bowl clean and was stealing fingerdabs of frosting from around the cake plates. Mrs. Thatcher had just parted Carrie's hair when one cake layer fell upside down on the kitchen floor.

Lonnie started screaming even before his mother smacked his bottom and sent him upstairs. Mrs. Thatcher leaned against the table, eyes closed, and fumbled a handkerchief from her apron pocket. For a moment Carrie thought she was crying but decided it was sweat she wiped away. There were dark patches of it on her mother's dress.

Carrie moved around the table to pick up the mess but her mother said, "Leave it. You'll get yourself dirty. Estrella!"

"I can just put a ribbon on my hair." Loose hair was a hot nuisance and Carrie hated it, but she felt she should make the offer. She was relieved when her mother shook her head and went on with the braiding. She was finished before Estrella began washing the floor.

"Now turn around," said Mrs. Thatcher.

Carrie turned as quickly as she dared and was approved. The instructions were always the same.

"Mind your manners. Don't forget to say please and thank you, and before you leave, be sure to thank Mrs. Dollingwood for a lovely evening."

"I will." Carrie bolted down the hall.

"Don't run!"

"I won't."

But she walked as fast as she could through the front door and across the street. Mrs. Dollingwood answered her knock and led her toward the parlor, which was never closed off in the Dollingwood house.

From upstairs Portia called, "Mama, is that Carrie?"

"Yes, dear."

"Come on up, Carrie."

Mrs. Dollingwood answered. "In a moment."

Carrie was sorry she'd hurried. Mr. Dollingwood came to the parlor door, an open copy of the *Epithet* in his hand.

After again thanking Carrie for her assistance he waved the newspaper and said, "Can you add anything to Weatherberry's self-serving ravings?"

Carrie guessed he meant the old article about the mummy. "No, sir."

She shifted nervously toward the stairs. Mrs. Dollingwood patted her shoulder, either to comfort her or to keep her still. Carrie couldn't decide which.

Mr. Dollingwood said, "Let me ask you this. Did my daughter appear rational and coherent before she enter . . . ah, approached the desiccated remains?"

What did he want her to say? A phrase of her mother's popped into Carrie's mind. "Well, she wasn't quite herself."

"There," he said to his wife. "She mustn't be left alone."

"Mary will be here," said Mrs. Dollingwood.

Portia called, louder, "Carrie."

Mrs. Dollingwood's hand pushed Carrie gently toward the stairs. "Don't let her get excited."

"And don't discuss this afternoon," said Mr. Dollingwood. "Keep her mind off it."

Both instructions were impossible, so Carrie said nothing. She did manage to keep from running up the stairs. Portia waited in the upstairs hall. She bustled Carrie into her bedroom, shut the door and leaned against it.

She shook her head. "Honestly, Carrie, you make it sound so dull. 'She wasn't quite herself.'"

"What else could I say?" Without lying, she meant.

"Something interesting. 'Her look was crazed, her steps unwilling. She groped her way forward, then her breath stopped, her brow paled and her limbs gave way.'"

Portia suited actions to her words and ended by tumbling among the lace and embroidered pillows heaped three deep along the bed's mahogany headboard. Carrie sat on the edge of the bed, careful not to crease the heavily fringed spread.

"What did the mummy say when he called you?" Portia's blank look was the only answer Carrie needed. "You didn't really faint."

"Swoon."

"You didn't, did you?"

Portia wound one of the pillow ribbons around her finger. "Somebody had to get us out of there."

"We could've walked out the way we went in."

"Not after Mr. Jay came downstairs, we couldn't."

"We could have told him we came to see the mummy and thanked him kindly."

"And tomorrow everybody in Stringtown

would've known. It would've been worse than Dr. Brewster's sister, and we can't leave town." There were tears in Portia's eyes.

Carrie sighed. "They'll still know."

"But they'll know we were forced to go in there. We were summoned." Portia clasped her hands demurely. "When one is called, one answers."

"Portia Dollingwood, you can't believe that."

"It's true!" Portia sat up. "Remember the séance? He touched me. Chickalimmy was calling me then, seeking to be heard."

"I wonder."

"But it's true!" Portia leaned forward, her eyes bright with excitement. "The very best people in San Francisco go to spiritists. Aunt Jennifer says the richest men have Madame Batashka consult the spirits for business advice."

"I know that. I just wonder if it was really Chickalimmy."

"Who else could it have been?"

Her brothers, thought Carrie, though she couldn't figure any way they could have gotten in and out of the sitting room without her seeing them.

"Us," she said. "Buzzer used to tease me about having spiders on my back. I'd feel them crawling, honest! But when I'd run to Mother, there wasn't anything there."

Portia looked offended. "Well, *I* don't imagine things. It was Chickalimmy touching me."

"Maybe." After all, professors had proven spiritism to be scientific and the Fox sisters had been about Portia's age when the spirits began rapping out messages for them. But Carrie knew how easily Portia got carried away. She said, "I think we should have another séance, just to be sure."

Portia clapped her hands. The excitement was back.

"Tonight," she said, then looked anxious. "If they decide to go."

She got up and tiptoed to the door, opened it and stuck out her head. After listening a long moment, she closed the door gently and returned to the bed, settling herself more sedately than she had before.

"I don't hear them talking, so they must have decided. Mother's probably in the kitchen telling Mary, and she'll be up here soon to tell us." Portia heaved a great sigh. "I'm always the last to know."

Carrie obliged by asking, "Know what?"

"About tonight. They've been invited to dinner at Mrs. Phillips's to meet the missionary from the Sandwich Islands. The one who's speaking at Marshall Hall tomorrow night. Papa says they should send their regrets and stay home with me, that I need attentive care. Mama says if they don't show their faces at the Phillipses', everyone will think they're ashamed of what happened this afternoon."

"Are they?"

"I don't know."

Carrie's finger traced a design in the weave of the spread. "Did you tell them why we went to see the mummy?"

"Of course. I was summoned."

Carrie looked up. There was no sign of teasing or theatricals. But Portia couldn't believe she'd been called. She must remember that Carrie had practically dragged her along to see the mummy. The table rap at the séance could have been Chickalimmy, but Carrie knew blamed well nobody had called them to see the mummy.

There was a tap on the door. Mrs. Dollingwood opened it and stepped in. Carrie wondered if Portia had heard some telltale creak of board and had spoken for her mother's ears. No, she would have signaled Carrie, and her look had been too solemn.

"It's much too warm up here," said Mrs. Dollingwood. "Let's go downstairs until dinner."

Portia said, "Aren't you dining with the missionary?"

"Your father will represent us. I'm having dinner with you." She included Carrie in her smile. "Now wash and come down. Your father must leave early and he wants to see you before he goes."

She left, closing the door behind her.

Portia made a face. "No séance."

"Are your parents going to hear the missionary tomorrow night?"

Portia shook her head.

"Mine are. Maybe you can come keep me company."

"Not if they think I'm not quite myself." Portia grinned. "Come on. We'll be proper young ladies."

They shared the Pear's soap and lavender water and went downstairs together. Mr. Dollingwood was ready to leave.

Along with his farewells he said, "With half the ladies in Stringtown parading on Main Street, I can't understand why none of them saw Portia and helped Carrie stop her."

"We're not going to discuss that any more this evening," Mrs. Dollingwood said firmly.

"I fear there will be no such restrictions at the Phillipses'. Good evening, my dears." He kissed his wife and daughter and bowed to Carrie.

When he'd gone, Mrs. Dollingwood sat down at the pianoforte and played songs with words they all knew. As they sang, Carrie noticed the songs were mostly happy ones, no "Tenting Tonight" or "Just Before the Battle, Mother."

Dinner was a fluffy egg dish, creamed potatoes and tiny Chinese peas. Since Mr. Dollingwood was absent, Mary had arranged the serving dishes around Mrs. Dollingwood's place. Portia's mother spooned food onto plates, passing the first to Carrie, the next to Portia and serving herself last.

Conversation was much like it was when Mr. Dollingwood was home, only Mrs. Dollingwood did most of the talking—about the lawless cowboys at Curly Bill's hangout, whether Arizona would achieve statehood and Mrs. Kelly's petition to stop cattle herds from being driven down Main Street.

Carrie thought the last was dangerously close to the afternoon's events. It must have reminded Portia, too, for while they both were receiving second helpings, Portia said, "Mr. Bender sold the Bon Ton."

Mrs. Dollingwood passed Carrie her refilled plate and took Portia's empty one. "Are you sure?"

"I heard it this afternoon at the Grand Palace. Everyone was talking about it. Mrs. Bender says it's because the desert is ruining her looks. She says if she has to spend another summer in Stringtown, she will absolutely die."

She finished the sweeping gestures that demonstrated Mrs. Bender's emotions and accepted her plate from her mother.

Mrs. Dollingwood smiled. "I feel sorry for your dinner partners, Portia. They will eventually seat you alone in a corner or tie your hands."

Portia giggled. "Hobble me like a horse. But isn't it romantic of Mr. Bender to sell the Bon Ton to please his beloved wife?"

Mrs. Dollingwood said, "I doubt if that's the reason he sold it."

Pleased at having something to contribute, Carrie said, "Perhaps he's going to take advantage of the Desert Land Act."

The Two-Bit Act, her father called it, for the government would sell a man as much as 640 acres of land at twenty-five cents an acre. The only requirement was that it be irrigated within three years. Father kept saying Essie's husband should resign his officer's commission and take advantage of the act.

"It's possible," said Mrs. Dollingwood, "but I think Mr. Bender just sold while he could ask the highest price. Once the mines start closing, businesses will be impossible to sell."

"But the mines aren't closing," said Carrie. "They're pumping the water out."

"Not as fast as it's coming in. Your father has ordered a larger pump, one of the largest made, I understand. But it may not be large enough." Mrs. Dollingwood shook her head. "It's like a Biblical curse, isn't it? All that water down there where we don't need or want it."

Portia said, "If the mines close, will we move to San Francisco?"

"That depends on your father."

Carrie couldn't enjoy the dessert, a really cool custard from the Dollingwood icebox. It was fine for Portia to chatter happily about the copper mines closing, but there wouldn't be any San Francisco for the Thatchers. The mining company would send Father to some other mine, someplace new where the town was still in tents. The prospect brought tears to her eyes.

They played word games after dinner. Most of Carrie's guesses were of things she would have to leave behind. She was relieved when Mr. Dollingwood came home before the lamps were lit and it was politely hinted that it was time for her to leave. She thanked Mrs. Dollingwood for a lovely evening.

Portia said, "I'll walk you down the steps."

"No farther." Mrs. Dollingwood's voice was unusually stern. "And no dawdling."

But they lingered on the porch long enough to hear Mr. Dollingwood say, in perfect imitation of Mrs. Kelly, "'. . . glassy-eyed as a sleepwalker and poor Carrie frantic to stop her. You could tell the poor child was not herself.' When I asked why she hadn't helped Carrie, she said she hadn't time to gather her forces. What the devil was she planning, an assault on the Rough-n-Ready?"

Mrs. Dollingwood murmured something.

Mr. Dollingwood said, "So does she. She's starting a petition to have the mummy destroyed. Everyone there signed it except me and I abstained only because I'm a lawyer."

Mrs. Dollingwood said something about Portia's whereabouts. Carrie rushed down the steps.

"See you after church," Portia called.

Carrie waved, but her mind was on Mrs. Kelly's lie. She couldn't possibly have seen Carrie and Portia. They'd used the saloon's back door. Was Mrs. Kelly so eager to have a finger in every pie that she'd lie?

Or, like Portia, had she talked herself into believing something that hadn't happened?

Thanks to Mrs. Kelly, Carrie was so involved in her thoughts that she stepped into the house unprepared. Father called her name and lit the lamp on the sitting room table. The whole family was waiting, facing the hall door like one of Judge Herker's hanging juries. Even Lonnie was there, silent and staring at her.

Her father hooked his thumbs in his vest and said, "What's this I hear?"

8

Frank Ainsley's Test

Buzzer grinned. Willie looked worried. Lonnie ran
to hug Carrie around the legs.

"You weren't teasing, were you?" he begged. "You
did see the mummy. You did."

Carrie patted his head. "Just a quick look. It isn't
much, honest."

The boy leaned against her. "I told you, Mother.
I told you, didn't I?"

"Half the town told me on my way home," said
Mr. Thatcher. "What I want to know is, how much
of it is true?"

Carrie didn't know what he'd heard. Willie looked

as if he'd like to help but he was too far away. Her
mother's face told her nothing. It was as blank and
stiff as the night Essie's officer had asked for her hand.
Carrie decided to risk keeping silent. As she'd hoped,
her father began leading her with questions, answering some himself and barely waiting for her answers
on others.

"First off, what were you doing in the Rough-n-
Ready? Sy Rayburn says you were dragged in by
that mummy."

Carrie was too astonished to answer.

"Well?" prompted her father. "Did that mummy
drag you in or didn't it?"

His tone frightened her. Buzzer stopped grinning
and that scared her even more. Portia was right. This
was far more serious than Miss Brewster's escapade.
But Carrie could no longer believe in Buzzer's spiders
and she wouldn't lie. Not unless she absolutely had to.

"Portia was dragged." Carrie had pulled her down
the alley and through the storeroom.

"You mean that thing got up, walked out on Main
Street and dragged the two of you inside?"

Lonnie went to lean on his mother's lap and be
comforted. Carrie envied him.

She told her father, "No, sir. I mean Portia said
he was calling and she had to answer. She just couldn't
help herself."

Mrs. Thatcher leaned forward. "Did you hear
anything?"

Carrie shook her head.

Her mother looked disappointed, but Father said, "Carrie's too sensible. I didn't raise any flibberty-jib with a head full of nonsense like some I could name." He lit a cigar, then asked, "If you didn't hear anything, how come you were inside the saloon?"

"I sort of got dragged along." That was true enough at the end when Portia was acting up.

"Carrie was trying to save her," said Mrs. Thatcher. "It was a noble Christian act. Are you sure you didn't hear something, Carrie?"

"I'm sure." She hadn't even heard Mr. Jay on the stairs.

Mr. Thatcher waved his cigar. "All right, now. Is it true that thing attacked Portia?" He sounded more like a lawyer than Mr. Dollingwood.

"All I know is, Portia fainted."

"Did you see it move?"

"No, sir."

"Then it didn't come here the other night, did it?" He looked certain of the answer. A sensible answer.

Carrie said, "Yes, it did."

Mr. Thatcher choked on his cigar.

Mrs. Thatcher smiled.

Lonnie said, "I told you, Mother. Didn't I?"

"Yes, dear."

Carrie hadn't Portia's lacy words, but she was in so far there was no getting out except by going ahead. She raised her chin and went on. "The mummy was here. It moved around the sitting room and rapped on the table. We heard it and felt it."

Lonnie chanted, "I told you, Mother."

Mrs. Thatcher tried to shush him. Mr. Thatcher paced the room, but Buzzer was grinning again and Carrie figured she was out of danger. Her knees felt too weak to hold her. She must have swayed.

Mother said, "Father, it's been a long day."

"Not long enough to figure this out." He sat at the table and smoothed out the *Epithet*. "If that Injun comes around again, you ask him about the water in the mines. If he tells you how to stop it, I'll buy that mummy from T. Jay and cover it with beads and feathers."

"Henry!"

"And stay out of places you don't belong," Mr. Thatcher told Carrie. "Next time you need a doctor, send one of the boys. You hear me?"

Carrie didn't bother explaining there'd been no boys to send. "Yes, sir."

Mrs. Thatcher stood up and took Lonnie's hand. "Come on, boys. Time for bed. You, too, Carrie."

Carrie led the way, moving quickly in the half dark. When they parted at the top of the stairs, her mother said softly, "You could have told me, Carrie."

"I know," Carrie lied.

Buzzer moaned like a ghost, sending Lonnie into screams and tears. It was a long time before the boys' room was quiet, but when Carrie went to listen on the stairs, her parents were still talking about spiritism.

"Rich and important people consult spiritists," her mother said. "Even royalty."

"And pay good money for the privilege," said her father. "But what can a dead nincompoop tell a smart businessman that he doesn't already know?"

Mrs. Thatcher said something about "the Beyond" and Mr. Thatcher grumbled about Portia's theatricals. Willie crept out to join Carrie. Buzzer followed, trailed by a whimpering Lonnie. Carrie went back to her room before Mother chased them.

Sunday breakfast was the same as other mornings only later and more rushed. Carrie passed along the platters of flapjacks, steaks, potatoes and eggs without taking any for herself.

"You're a growing girl," her mother told her. "You must eat."

"Yeah," said Buzzer, "you got to keep your spirit up."

He and Father thought it was funny. Willie looked at Carrie with sympathy. She took a bowl of oatmeal and a piece of pie so she'd have something to put her attention on. Over her mother's objections, she cleared the table for Estrella, who kept the kitchen table between them and stared at Carrie as if she'd grown a second head.

At the thought of church Carrie's stomach threatened to return the dried apple pie. She fought the nausea. Sickness for her wasn't ribboned pillows and chilled custards. She might escape the stares and questions at church but she'd spend the day in her room being dosed with sulfur and molasses and bitter tea. She sighed and went upstairs to get ready, taking so much time and trouble that she passed Mother's inspection the first try. Her brothers didn't.

For once, Father didn't seem to mind waiting, nor did he set his usual brisk pace when they finally started. He liked to talk business before and after services, but they were among the last to arrive at church. Everyone was already seated.

The aisle looked longer than tomorrow. Carrie thought of Portia in the Presbyterian church which was larger and had more members. She guessed what Portia was doing and decided to try it, to use what Father called Portia's fancy nonsense. She'd imagine herself royalty among commoners.

At first it was hard not to imagine she was going to the guillotine, but she kept her head up and her royal image firmly in mind. By the time she slipped into the pew she felt like a duchess being presented at an unfriendly court. She held onto the feeling, wafting her palmetto fan regally, until the second sentence of Reverend Pritchard's sermon on the weakness of the flesh.

"But we know," he said, "that the spirit is willing."

Buzzer wasn't the only one who sniggered. Carrie wished she could melt away and the puddle evaporate. She hoped Lonnie would start acting up or ask to be taken to the privy. Mother usually asked Carrie to take him out, and this time she'd go straight on home. But Lonnie sat lost in a dream world, whispering to weird creatures he shaped from his handkerchief.

The services ended and the line formed to shake

Reverend Pritchard's hand. Having a front pew put the Thatchers last in line. When they left the church, the men had already grouped to talk business or politics, the women to decide whose turn it was to invite the minister to dinner. The children were racing and teasing in toned-down Sunday fashion. All stopped to watch the Thatchers. Carrie felt like a curiosity in a circus parade.

For the first time Carrie could remember, her parents didn't stop to talk. They nodded and called greetings, but they marched past the staring Methodists and down the dirt street toward home. They arrived before Estrella took the chicken out of the oven. Carrie went straight to her room, threw herself across the bed and cried.

They were ashamed of her. Her parents found her a black sheep, what the magazines called an "embarrassment." The thought that they might now be glad to send her away brought no comfort.

Portia claimed it was the starers who were embarrassed. An unusual number of people had selected Third Street for their Sunday stroll and Portia had asked to spend the afternoon on the Thatcher back porch. It was shady and cool, and though it lacked a swing, today it offered more privacy than her own porch.

"Mama says they are confronted by a spiritual phenomenon," said Portia, "and they don't know how to act."

"And that makes them embarrassed," said Carrie.

She was sitting on the bottom step tracing squares inside of squares in the dirt with the shoe-cleaning stick. Portia stood beside her watching Estrella swamp the cooler.

"Yes," said Portia. "People are always embarrassed when they don't know how to behave."

From under the mesquite tree, Lonnie bawled, "Mother! Somebody took my stick!"

"Oh, Christmas," said Carrie. "How can he miss one little stick?"

Lonnie charged the steps, stopping when he saw Carrie's drawing tool. "You did! You broke the corral and the horses all ran away."

"Here, take it."

He trotted back to the shade.

Portia said, "Papa says people are just waiting for somebody to tell them what to think."

"I wish that somebody would hurry up."

Estrella went inside the house. Portia sat down beside Carrie.

"We've been doing the séance all wrong. We're supposed to have a control." Portia arranged herself slantways over three steps. "Do I look languorous?"

Carrie said, "What's a control?"

"A spirit that gives and takes messages from the Other Side, the spirit world."

"Why can't the spirits speak for themselves?"

"I don't know. They just don't. Aunt Jennifer says

Madame Batashka goes into a trance and then the control speaks through her, answering questions from the Beyond. And guess what? Madame Batashka's control is an Indian! I think that's what Chickalimmy is, a control."

"Then maybe he can tell us where Geronimo is."

"Spirits don't send that kind of message."

"Why not?"

"It isn't the kind of thing people want to know."

"It's what General Crook wants to know. And Wells Fargo and the Marshall Freight Line."

Portia giggled. "And Papa. He says Stringtown summers are tough enough without having Mama and me suffering through them, too."

Carrie tried to get her back on the trail. "What kind of questions do spirits answer?"

"I didn't get to hear that part." Portia bent over her turned-up hem. "I do believe this skirt should be let down, don't you?"

"Were you eavesdropping again?"

"I just happened to be sitting on the stairs last evening when Mama and Papa were talking."

Carrie pretended disapproval. "Young ladies don't eavesdrop."

"Then they're going to be pretty dumb, because nobody ever tells them anything."

"A true message, Madame Dollinska."

While they giggled and did silly versions of Madame Batashka, the boys came home. Willie tried to settle on the steps, but Buzzer's "Come on, Willie" got him back on his feet and into the kitchen. Estrella sent them out. Willie sat beside Portia, smiling up at her. Buzzer stomped down the steps to stand in front of Carrie.

"I need some more jars," he told her. "Estrella won't let me get them."

Carrie pretended great interest in a circling buzzard. Keeping her voice bored, she said, "You break Mother's good canning jars, she'll skin you."

"We ain't going to break them."

She wondered what they were going to do with them, but if she asked, she'd lose her advantage. She hummed and watched the buzzard. Portia was telling Willie what a nice Southern gentleman Frank Ainsley was and how he bowed and spoke whenever the water sprinkler passed her house. As if Willie cared, but that solemn gaze and kind smile got people to tell him all kinds of strange things. Carrie thought it was like talking to a dog, only better.

At last Buzzer said, "You get the jars for me."

"What makes you think Estrella will let me take them?"

Buzzer grinned. "She will."

Carrie yawned. The buzzard landed.

"Come on, Carrie. You get me those jars and I'll tell you something." He fidgeted through a short silence, then, "Something you and Miss Darlingwood had better know quick."

He made it sound urgent and serious, but with Buzzer Carrie could never be sure. She decided to wait a little longer.

"Something you better know about that mummy," he added.

Portia stopped talking in mid-sentence and prodded Carrie with the toe of her shoe. After that show of interest there wasn't any use bargaining to be told the news *before* getting the jars. Carrie glared at Portia and hoped she wasn't being flimflammed.

Buzzer was right about one thing. Estrella didn't stop her. She turned from her pot-scrubbing to watch, but didn't ask a single question. That didn't mean she wouldn't tell Mother, giving Carrie some explaining to do. Carrie kept that in mind when deciding how many jars to take. The seven she could manage were too many. Four might give Buzzer an excuse to call off the deal. She took five, gave Estrella a smile that wasn't returned and marched outside.

"Just five?" said Buzzer. "I need more than that."

"What for?"

"Get me five more jars and I might tell you."

"You haven't paid for these yet." And Carrie wasn't giving them up until he had.

Buzzer grinned at Portia. "Your Pa and Doc Brewster mixed words today. Doc said that mummy's been dead a hundred years and if it wanted to talk it would've done it before now. He said females are high-strung and overdeveloped in the imagination.

And then Mr. Dollingwood said. . . . What was it he said, Willie?"

"Sir, you are impugning my daughter's integrity," Willie said carefully. He looked up at Portia. "That means Doc said you were lying. Mr. Weatherberry told me."

"I've been insulted," cried Portia, sprawling across the stairs in her languorous pose. "My good name has been sullied and besmirched."

Willie nodded. "That's what your father said, all except for besmirched."

"Then what?" Carrie prompted.

Buzzer shrugged. "The words got longer and louder and people stopped to listen. Not as many as when the girls from the Rough-n-Ready and the Silver Dollar got to pulling hair, but they collected quite a crowd for Sunday. Sold all my papers in no time."

Portia moaned. If she hadn't already been languoring all over the steps, she'd probably have swooned. Carrie stepped over her legs and up the stairs as if returning the jars. Buzzer grabbed her skirt.

"Hold on, Carrie. There's more. Why don't you let Willie hold some of those jars?"

"What you've told me so far isn't worth a hoot in a barrel."

"It is, too," wailed Portia. "I'm mortified."

"Don't worry. Frank Ainsley's got everyone to agree to a scientific test." Buzzer grabbed two jars and handed them to Willie. The others started slipping and Buzzer got those, too. "Come on, Willie!"

Since she'd gotten herself on the up-step side of Portia, Carrie hadn't a hope of catching the boys. She called after them, "What kind of test?"

Buzzer answered, "To see if Miss Poah-shyah's been impugned."

Willie hung back, watching the girls.

"Come on," Buzzer yelled. "Fourth of July's getting close and fireworks don't come free in Arbuckle's Coffee."

The boys ran past the privy and into the desert.

"I'm a damosel in distress," said Portia. "And Frank Ainsley's rescuing me. I told you he was a Southern gentleman."

"If he's a gentleman, why is he putting you to a public test?"

"To prove my honor lily white, pure as driven snow." Portia sat up so she could gesture. "Proud she stands, acclaimed by all, disimpugned and sully-free."

"Suppose you fail?"

Portia stared at her.

"The test," Carrie reminded her. "Suppose they want Chickalimmy to speak?"

"Why, then he'll speak."

"But suppose he doesn't?"

"Carrie Thatcher, are you impugning my honor?"

Carrie tried hard not to impugn and still get Portia to think seriously about the test, but Portia went home in a tiff. It didn't last, though. When Mr. Dollingwood called on Carrie's father, Portia came along. The men closed themselves in the parlor, but Portia told Carrie and Mrs. Thatcher what they were talking about.

Frank Ainsley's test had been arranged for Tuesday morning, before the worst heat of the day. Morning would also give Mr. Weatherberry time to write the story for Tuesday's *Epithet*, and the Grand Palace was expecting a large crowd for the noon meal in return for the use of its lobby. Mr. Dollingwood hoped the time suited the Thatchers because he wanted Carrie to be present, too.

"I insisted on it," said Portia.

Carrie wished she hadn't.

The visit was short because Mrs. Dollingwood was home, sick with a headache. According to Portia, the headache had started coming on when Mrs. Smedley called to tell Mrs. Dollingwood about the séance, and it wasn't expected to go away until Tuesday after-noon.

"I won't be able to come over tonight," Portia whispered as they left.

Carrie's parents didn't go to hear the missionary after all. Mrs. Thatcher said it was too windy and the dust would ruin her blue summer cashmere, but Carrie suspected she'd caught Mrs. Dollingwood's headache.

Monday was washday. Estrella spent the best part

of the day outside with tubs and washboard. Cleaning, bed-making, potato-peeling and washing dishes fell to Carrie, her mother helping indoors and out. It seemed most of the day was spent either getting a meal ready or cleaning up after it. Carrie didn't get over to the Dollingwoods', but while she was peeling potatoes for supper Portia came around the house with the *Epithet*.

"Listen!" She sat on the steps, accepted a slice of raw potato to munch and opened the newspaper on her knees. "Mr. Weatherberry says the test will be 'a demonstration of the scientific principles of extra-sensory survival. The spirit will at last be weighed and evaluated.' What does that mean?"

"They're going to do something to the mummy. Assay it or something." Carrie was vastly relieved. Also puzzled. "Then why do they want us there?"

"For our grace and charm. That's what Mr. Weatherberry calls us, 'graceful and charming.' See?"

He had. Not just Portia but Carrie, too. "The graceful and charming daughters of Mr. Benjamin Dollingwood and Mr. Henry W. Thatcher." Carrie smiled and picked up another potato.

Portia said, "What are you wearing tomorrow?"

"I don't know." For the first time, Carrie felt an interest in Portia's fashion prattle, but she was soon bored with the virtues of ribbon and satin loops. She was glad when the boys came home and interrupted.

Buzzer went straight inside but Willie sat down and stared at Portia.

"It's all that grace and charm," Carrie told her. "He can't resist it."

Willie took a painted tube from inside his shirt and handed it to Portia. She put it to her eye.

"It's a kaleidoscope," she said.

Buzzer said, "It's the Tube of a Thousand Flowers."

"Who said so?"

"Wing Lee."

Portia handed back the kaleidoscope. "What are you doing talking to Wing Lee?"

"He's my friend." Willie looked hurt.

Carrie said, "Did Wing Lee give you the Tube of a Thousand Flowers?"

Willie nodded.

"Why?"

"He's going away."

Prying with questions, Carrie finally learned that Wing Lee was leaving Stringtown in three weeks and was giving his friends farewell presents.

Portia sniffed. "How many friends can Wing Lee have?"

Willie said quietly, "Me."

"What about the other Chinese?" asked Carrie.

"They're relatives, I think."

Carrie took a peek in the kaleidoscope and handed it back to her brother. "Better put it away before Lonnie sees it. You can hide it on top of my wardrobe if you like."

Willie nodded and left.

"Your brother talks to very peculiar people," said Portia. "What's the matter? You aren't still worried about Frank Ainsley's old test, are you?"

"No. Something worse. The Marshall Mine is closing after the Fourth of July."

"Where did you hear that?"

"Right here. You told me yourself that Wing Lee has been with Mrs. Marshall's family forever."

Portia nodded. "I heard it at one of Mama's socials. But Wing Lee could be leaving without the Marshalls."

"I doubt it. And the Marshalls wouldn't be leaving unless they were closing the mine. The Marshall Mine's had more water trouble than any of the others. It's worked at a lower level. And three weeks is just after the Fourth of July." Carrie nodded. "It figures."

"I guess they don't want to put all those men out of work before the holiday. That would certainly spoil the parade and everything, wouldn't it?"

Carrie thought it more likely Mr. Marshall wanted to sell his interest in the bank, the Grand Palace and the Marshall Freight Line before the panic started. With lots of strangers in town for the Fourth, nobody would notice his buyers. She remembered Father telling of something similar years ago. Carrie sighed heavily.

Portia said, "One mine closing doesn't mean the end of Stringtown."

"Not right away." The Thatchers would be

around as long as the company made a profit from the mine, but sooner or later pumping the water would cost too much.

Portia chattered about the Fourth of July parade and how it would serve Emma Lou Smedley right not to have anyone to wave to.

"I don't think we'd better say anything about this," Carrie warned her. "Mr. Marshall might be awful mad."

"Raging and vengeful," agreed Portia. "I won't say a word, I promise. See you tomorrow at your graceful and charming best."

At least the test was no longer a danger, not if all Frank Ainsley planned was to weigh the mummy.

But when they walked into the Grand Palace lobby next morning, there was no mummy. Just a small polished wood box and a glass dome.

9

Chickalimmy's Voice

There were a lot of people in the lobby, all standing near the walls. Only Mr. Weatherberry, Dr. Brewster and Judge Herker stood with Frank Ainsley by the table in the center of the room. It was as if the Brussels carpet were a stage or royal ground. Carrie felt a thrill of excitement as Mr. Reeter led the Thatchers, Portia and Mr. Dollingwood forward.

A chair was brought for Mrs. Thatcher. Carrie feared Lonnie would begin fussing about the missing mummy, but he leaned against his mother and was quiet.

Mr. Dollingwood told the doctor, "There are too many people here, Daniel."

"Right," muttered Buzzer. "With all of these watching, who's going to buy a newspaper?"

Carrie glared at him.

"This is a scientific investigation," Mr. Dollingwood continued, "not a paid exhibition. Can't we move to a private room?"

Frank Ainsley said, "The more witnesses, the stronger the proof, and it is Miss Portia's integrity at stake today."

Portia lowered her eyes modestly but gave Carrie a gleeful smile. Carrie frowned back, warning her that something dreadful was coming. She felt it in her stomach.

"He's right," said Mr. Thatcher. "The more people here, the better."

He didn't add what he'd said at breakfast, that he expected to see a fiasco.

Judge Herker said, "I never liked a closed court."

Mr. Dollingwood agreed to remain in the lobby.

"Let's get on with it," said Dr. Brewster, then immediately insisted on a different table, going into the bar to select it himself. Mr. Weatherberry and the judge accompanied him to be sure the new table wasn't tampered with.

"We must be impartial," said Judge Herker.

While waiting for the new table, Carrie had a chance to steal glances at the onlookers. All the women from church and the Shakespeare Society were there and quite a few men in spite of the awkward time. Even the Marshalls had come to watch. But there was little talking and the silence made her nervous. She remembered what Portia had said about people waiting to be told what to think. She dreaded what was coming, but Portia gazed at the carved ceiling with the look she wore when playing Mary in the Christmas tableaux.

The long polished table was replaced by a heavy square one. Dr. Brewster looked happier, the judge slightly flushed. Mr. Weatherberry began taking notes. Frank Ainsley left the group of men to stand on the opposite side of the table.

"Mr. Thatcher, sir," he said, "will you assemble the scales for us?"

Carrie's father looked startled, then pleased. He stepped to the table, opened the box and removed a set of small scales used to weigh gold dust. The pans were so delicately balanced that when empty, the slightest air movement set them bobbing.

"Just a minute," said Dr. Brewster. "Where'd these scales come from?"

"From my bank, and nobody has opened the box since I brought them."

There was rustling as people craned to find the speaker, then recognized Mr. Marshall.

Carrie was astonished. Not only had Frank Ainsley thought of everything, he'd persuaded the most important people in town to help. Why? And what was it all leading to?

Frank Ainsley stood relaxed behind the table. In his brushed frock coat and embroidered vest, one could almost mistake him for the Southern gentleman Portia imagined him to be.

"The glass dome," he said, "came directly from Judge Herker's parlor, lent us by his gracious wife." He bowed to where she stood beside Mrs. Marshall.

"I can vouch for the dome," said Judge Herker.

Dr. Brewster said, "I prefer to examine it."

Almost every parlor had one like it covering a dried-flower arrangement or small stuffed birds. The doctor held it in one hand and ran the other around the inside, the rim and the outside. He nodded and placed it on the table.

"Gentlemen," said Frank Ainsley, "will you agree this scale can detect the movement of any being, no matter how insubstantial?"

The small pans hadn't stopped their gentle up-and-down movement since being set up by Mr. Thatcher.

"If you can cut off the draft," said Carrie's father. "Is that what the jar's for?"

"Yes, sir. I will place the dome over the scales and the spirit will be summoned. If the scales move, will you gentlemen agree that only a spirit could have moved them?"

There was a rustling as everyone came forward. Carrie sneaked a glance at Portia. She was staring at the scales, her face pale and tense. If she swooned, there was sure to be someone to catch her.

The men took time and short speeches to agree that movement of the scales under the dome would signify the presence of a spirit.

"Miss Portia," Frank Ainsley bowed to her. "I regret we were refused the presence of the spirit's physical remains, but I understand that isn't necessary. You can summon the spirit from a distance."

He paused. When Portia didn't answer, he added, "As indeed it has summoned you."

Eyes still on the scales, Portia said, "If Carrie helps me, I can."

Now if she failed, she could blame it on Carrie. It was the sort of weaseling Carrie expected from Buzzer, not her friend. She was almost as angry as she was scared.

Mrs. Thatcher nudged her forward. "Go on, dear."

People crowded toward the table until Dr. Brewster said, "Halt! Any heavy movement or vibration might be conducted to the scale. Please remain still and silent until the test is finished."

Frank Ainsley couldn't have been as calm as he appeared. He wiped his forehead with a handkerchief and returned it to the pocket inside the tail of his coat. Carrie wished for a drink of water. Frank Ainsley picked up the glass dome.

"If you gentlemen will make way for the ladies." He waited until the men had moved a few steps from the table, placed the dome over the scales and stepped back. The pans stilled. "All is ready, Miss Portia. Miss Carrie."

Portia held out her hand. With everyone watching, there was nothing Carrie could do but take it. Holding tight, they stepped forward, stopping an arm's length from the table.

Portia took a deep breath and began. "Come, thou spirit, we beseech thee. Come, we beg you. Give us signal of your presence."

The pans remained steady.

"Give us a sign, dread spirit." Portia's voice broke. She squeezed Carrie's hand.

Desperately, Carrie said, "Show yourself!"

One side of the scale dipped. The pans rocked gently. The crowd sighed.

Carrie let go of Portia's hand and stared. There was a muffled sound from Buzzer. He sat on the carpet by Mother's chair, arms crossed on his knees and the lower part of his face hidden in them. Carrie knew he was laughing. She looked at Frank Ainsley but he was serious and intent on Portia. She stood like a sleep-walker, arms outstretched and eyes closed. The murmurs of the crowd died away.

Portia announced, "My name is Chickalimmy, chief of the Chickamaugas. I gottum message."

"I knew it," cried Mrs. Kelly. "It's that heathen spell again."

Frank Ainsley raised his hand. "Hush! She's in a trance. We must not waken her."

Mr. Dollingwood whispered, "Daniel, is she all right?"

"She's fine." Dr. Brewster was watching the scale, which continued to bob erratically.

Portia continued. "The dread Apache puttum curse on the mines of Stringtown. Callum water from all the earth. Higher it rise, ever higher. Mines close!"

There was movement and noise from the crowd. Portia raised her voice. "First mine close soon! Only waiting past Fourth of July!"

There was stunned silence, then an upsurge of voices. Only those around the table heard the last of Chickalimmy's message.

"Mar . . . Marshall . . . ooooh." Portia collapsed gracefully into Judge Herker's arms.

"Hot Jupiter!" Mr. Weatherberry stepped over her outstretched legs and headed toward Mr. Marshall who was edging toward the door. Mr. Dollingwood tried to carry Portia to a couch but people milled and swirled through the lobby. There were several calls for smelling salts.

Above the din came Mr. Thatcher's "Carrie!"

The space around the table had filled with people. Carrie pushed through them to where Father stood behind Mrs. Thatcher's chair. Buzzer and Willie were gone. Lonnie stood by his mother, one hand fending off bustles. Mrs. Thatcher looked as if she might need smelling salts.

It was better after Carrie arrived. People began to

circle the Thatchers, leaving an open area. It was a while before Carrie understood it was because of her. Women stopped to exchange words with Mrs. Thatcher but they kept looking at Carrie. It was like riding in the surrey with Portia.

Mrs. Smedley was chatting when Mr. Thatcher told Lonnie, "Come on, son. I'll sneak you in for a peek at the mummy."

Lonnie shook his head.

"Don't you want to see the mummy?"

"I saw the mummy," Lonnie said to his mother's lap. "Two."

"Twice?" said Mrs. Thatcher.

Lonnie held up two fingers.

"Twice!" said Mrs. Smedley. "Of course, we knew about the one time. Our Frank saw the ghost on Third Street the night of the séance. I hadn't heard about the other time."

The night of the séance Carrie and Portia had tiptoed around the boys' room wearing that lumpy face mask. Carrie was sure Lonnie meant he'd seen two mummies.

"If you ask me," Mrs. Smedley went on, "it's Carrie he likes. It's her house he went to and he didn't jump until she called. I don't know why he chose to speak through the Dollingwood girl. Of course, that phrenologist did say she was loquacious, though there are some who'd call it something different. Carrie, now, is a nice, sensible girl."

Carrie was beginning to hate that word. Sensible girls peeled potatoes and made everything sound dull while flibberty-jibs swooned and rode in surreys. If Mrs. Smedley knew the truth about the girls getting into the Rough-n-Ready, she wouldn't think Carrie was sensible.

When the woman had said her farewells and left, Mrs. Thatcher said, "She's right, you know. About the mummy. It's you he likes."

Carrie stared at her. "But it's Portia who calls him."

"And you he answers."

Mr. Thatcher looked at his pocket watch. "I can't loaf any longer. You sure you don't want to see that mummy, son?"

Lonnie shook his head. "I want to see the horses."

"Be good, don't give Mother any trouble and I'll walk you down to the livery stable after supper."

Mrs. Thatcher stood and they moved toward the door. The lobby had cleared. The roar of voices now came from the bar. Portia sat on a couch between her father and Dr. Brewster, who seemed to be having a heated debate. Portia gave a helpless shrug. Carrie smiled.

Twice Mr. Thatcher was asked if the company was closing the mine. The first time they all waited while he explained the new pump. The second time he told Mrs. Thatcher, "Don't wait for me. And I won't be home for dinner."

Mrs. Thatcher quickly led Carrie and Lonnie out

the door. Main Street looked like Saturday afternoon. Mrs. Kelly and three friends blocked the walk in front of the Grand Palace. They greeted Mrs. Thatcher while smiling and staring at Carrie.

"I'm going to ask for the mail," Mrs. Thatcher told Carrie. "Take Lonnie home before he fusses."

Carrie took her brother's hand. As she led him across the street she heard Mrs. Kelly telling how she'd tried to help Carrie hold Portia back from entering the Rough-n-Ready. The sunny side of Main Street had fewer people and there was no one on Third Street except old Mrs. McPhersen calling her old yellow tomcat.

The house was quiet except for Estrella's singing. Carrie took Lonnie upstairs, helped him into his play clothes, changed her dress and sat down on the bed. She stared out at the hills, each topped by the wood frame of a mine shaft and swollen with heaps of slag.

There really was a Chickalimmy. Right up until the scale moved Carrie had suspected it was just another of Portia's theatricals. That's what came of being sensible. She'd also been angry with Portia, thinking she'd planned a way to blame Carrie if the scale didn't move. But if Mother and Mrs. Smedley were right, Portia had really needed her help. Maybe when Portia went to San Francisco again, the dome and scales and Carrie would go along.

She heard Mother come home and the sound of a meal being prepared. Estrella ironed on Tuesday and

Carrie expected to be called to help with dinner, but no one disturbed her daydreams until Willie tapped on the door and asked to get his kaleidoscope.

He sat on the bed and they took turns changing the colored shapes. While Carrie was looking, he said, "Will you make Buzzer let Colossus go?"

Carrie lowered the tube. "Who's Colossus?"

He spoke so softly Carrie had to strain to hear. "Tony Ramirez says he's the biggest tarantula he's ever seen, and smart, too. He comes when I tap and rides on my arm and Buzzer said we wouldn't match him, just keep him in Frank's room with the rest because Mother doesn't like bugs. Then the big centipedes killed two tarantulas last night and the scorpions don't want to fight and Buzzer says if we're going to draw some of the crowd from the Rough-n-Ready tonight, we got to match Colossus. Will you make Buzzer let him go?"

"You mean you've been holding cockfights, only with bugs?" She didn't need Willie's nod. It all fit, the clothesline pole, the jars, the expeditions after dark. "What all have you been catching for Frank Ainsley?"

"Tarantulas, scorpions, stuff like that. Frank wants to match a cat and a rattlesnake Saturday but me and Buzzer aren't ready to tackle a rattler."

"I should hope not! Where are you holding these matches?"

"First off it was just a warm-up for the cockfights

last Saturday. Buzzer thought it up. Then Portia made the mummy real popular and Frank gave the Silver Dollar the notion to hold the matches every night." He rolled the kaleidoscope back and forth on the bed.

"Inside the saloon?" whispered Carrie.

Willie nodded and whispered back, "You won't tell Mother?"

"No." It was going to be much too useful as a threat to Buzzer.

"And you'll save Colossus?"

"Why don't you just steal him out of Frank Ainsley's room and let him go?"

"Buzzer would just find him again unless you make him promise." He said something about Portia, but so softly Carrie had to ask him to repeat it. "I said I was going to ask Portia not to let Chickalimmy talk any more, then maybe the Silver Dollar wouldn't need the matches and we could save all the spiders and things."

So that's why he'd been mooning around Portia. Poor Willie. He hadn't much sense if he thought Portia would silence Chickalimmy even if she could.

"I'll save Colossus for you," Carrie promised. "It will be my parting gift before I conquer the nabobs of San Francisco."

It didn't sound half as grand as when Portia imagined something, but Carrie thought she'd improve with practice. Willie was a good audience, wide-eyed and silent. Carrie daydreamed aloud until Buzzer yelled from the foot of the stairs, "Dinner's ready."

Not only did he call, he waited for them. Carrie felt quite grand until she swept past him and he muttered, "Are you ever dumb."

10

Carrie's Million and One

Carrie turned on him. "What do you mean, dumb?"

"Letting prissy Miss Darlingwood steal all the glory. You can get rich being a spiritist." He walked past her. "Come on. I'm hungry."

Carrie followed him into the dining room. Mrs. Thatcher had put all the platters on the table and was waiting for Carrie, just as if she were company. After dinner she refused Carrie's help with the dishes.

"You make Estrella nervous," she said. "No telling what stories she's been spreading in Mextown. If she leaves, I might not get anyone else. Why don't you go outside and read?"

She didn't wait to be told twice. She got the book Tom had sent for her birthday, *Travels in Hindustan*. She'd already read it twice, but it had lots of detailed pictures and descriptions. She was hunting tigers from the back of an elephant when Portia came flying around the house waving the *Epithet*.

"Where have you been?" She plunked down beside Carrie. "Mr. Weatherberry calls the test uncontestable and says no scientific nabob can fault it. He also calls me 'the charming and comely Miss Dollingwood.'"

Carrie took the newspaper, folded to the article about the test. Most of it was devoted to the preliminaries and a list of the onlookers. Portia was called comely and charming when Chickalimmy spoke through her, prophesying the closing of a mine after the Fourth of July. Carrie wasn't called anything but Miss Thatcher. The article said the Dandy Mine, one of the smallest, was indeed closing after the Fourth of July. Though it was learned that Mr. Marshall was relieving himself of too many business interests, he had no plans to close the Marshall Mine. Carrie knew what Buzzer and Father would say to that.

Portia took back the newspaper. "I'm sending this to Aunt Jennifer. Won't she be surprised!" She giggled. "But not half as surprised as I was."

"*You?*" Carrie remembered the clutching hand and the voice breaking after only a few sentences. Portia had been scared. "You didn't really believe in Chicka-limmy!"

"I do now."

"But you didn't. How could you agree to a test? How could you let us get up in front of all those people knowing we were going to make a spectacle of ourselves?"

"I thought you'd manage something."

"*Me?*" Carrie jumped to her feet. She'd never been so furious. Portia tried to get her to sit down. She refused, but she did lower her voice. "Why me?"

"Well, I thought maybe it was you knocking on the table that night."

"I wouldn't do a thing like that."

"I know, but I thought it might have been."

"It wasn't." Carrie sat down. But it might have been the boys. No, not after what happened this morning. "It's spooky."

Portia nodded and stood up. "I have to go. Mama still has her headache, and Mary quit. Things are in sort of a mess. What's funny?"

"The way we're turned around. Mother told me to come out here and read."

Portia made a face. "I think Chickalimmy likes you better than me."

Father didn't think so. He told Mrs. Thatcher at supper, "If he likes Carrie so much, how come Portia's doing his talking? Doc Brewster says people pay more to consult a spiritist than they do a doctor.

Though it beats me how an Indian gets smart soon as he dies."

"They must know something," said Mrs. Thatcher. "Spiritists are consulted by royalty."

Mr. Thatcher snorted. "Royalty doesn't know beans about Indians."

Carrie thought wistfully of being sought by kings and earls. The tiger hunt couldn't hold her attention. She drifted around the yard until it was late enough for the Dollingwoods to have eaten, then went over to help Portia with the dishes. They spent so much time practicing the curtsy and walking with a train that it was dark when Carrie went home. Crossing the street, she scared a coyote and hoped it hadn't found Mrs. McPhersen's cat.

Next afternoon Mrs. Smedley called. Carrie didn't find out until she'd left that the visit was to invite Carrie to the Sunday Evening Theosophical Society.

"They want to hear from Chickalimmy," Mrs. Thatcher told her.

Carrie panicked. "I can't! Not without Portia."

"I'm sure you could if you put your mind to it. However, Cora's speaking to Mrs. Dollingwood now. She came here first." Mrs. Thatcher smiled. "Imagine, before the Dollingwoods. If we both work on your new dress, we can finish it by Sunday."

"It's too hot to sew."

"We'll work in the parlor. It's cooler in there."

It wasn't much cooler, but being offered use of the

parlor like any other room flattered Carrie into agreeing. She looked forward to ushering Portia in there, but when Portia ran over to talk about Mrs. Smedley's invitation, she refused to come inside.

"I have to watch for the ice man," she told Carrie. "Mama's cold compresses are using so much ice Papa had to ask for a special delivery. Isn't it exciting about Sunday night?"

"Do you think we ought to practice?" Carrie would feel easier if she knew what to expect.

"Here he comes."

They walked slowly across the street debating the risk of another séance.

"Maybe there's only just so much power," Portia said. "And when we use it up, Chickalimmy won't be able to speak."

The possibility gave Carrie a fresh worry. "All the more reason for another séance, to be sure we're still in touch."

Portia agreed. "But not too close to Sunday, so the power has time to build up again."

When the wagon stopped beside them, they'd decided Friday night was close enough but not too close. Lonnie came running to beg a sliver of ice and Carrie got a piece for herself. She sent Lonnie in the house for newspaper. He was back in no time, fearful that his ice had melted away. Carrie brushed off the sawdust and wrapped the bottoms of the slivers with newspaper so they could be held like licorice sticks.

Lonnie headed for the mesquite tree. Carrie followed, postponing her return to seam stitching.

"You leave my corral alone," Lonnie warned.

They sat together, letting the ice numb lips and tongue. Carrie crunched the last bit and tossed the soggy paper away. Lonnie moved his stick horses, talking softly as he played. The boys came home. While Buzzer went inside, Willie came to squat beside Carrie. His eyes were large and troubled.

"You going to talk to Buzzer?" he asked.

"Not now." Carrie nodded at Lonnie, who'd stopped his murmuring to listen. "Little pitchers. Why'd you come home?"

"Letter from Essie. You going to talk to Buzzer today?"

"I'll try."

Buzzer must have delivered the letter to Mother in the parlor and gone out the front door. He stepped around the front corner of the house to yell, "Come on, Willie. You know that dumb Injun won't stop for me."

"Is Apache Sam back?" She grinned. "Couldn't he find Geronimo either?"

"He wasn't looking. Geronimo's been in Mexico more than a month."

"How do you know?"

"Apache Sam told me."

"Then who's been raiding and killing around here?"

"Chihuahua."

"Willie!" yelled Buzzer. "Come on! You want a ride or don't you?"

From the sitting room window Mother called, "Carrie, do you want this dress or don't you?"

With a sigh Carrie pushed herself to her feet and walked toward the house with Willie. The water sprinkler was creeping down Third Street.

Carrie said, "Why'd Apache Sam come back if he's so afraid of the mummy?"

Willie flushed. "That's not why he left. I heard T. Jay arguing about who fights the worst, a Indian or a Chinese. Apache Sam's the only Indian in Stringtown, so when they started making bets I got scared. I told Apache Sam and he made himself scarce."

Buzzer came up to them. "And you'll get made scarce if you don't stop messing in people's deals." He pushed Willie toward the street.

"Carrie," called Mrs. Thatcher.

She shrugged helplessly at Willie, promised, "After supper," and went inside. Mother was so tight-lipped and snappish that Carrie wondered what was in Essie's letter. She knew better than to ask. Letters were never read or discussed with the children until Father had seen them. Carrie sweated and sewed in silence.

After supper Willie took Lonnie and a canning jar down to the riverbed. Carrie thought Lonnie was a little young for spider-catching, but stopping him would have brought on a screaming spell. Besides,

Willie did it so Carrie could be alone at the mesquite tree with Buzzer. He climbed the branches and dropped bits of dried branches down on her.

Before she could bring up Willie and Colossus, Buzzer said, "The Dandy Mine's closing Friday. Jed Hopkins says since Chickalimmy told on him, there's no sense hanging on till after the Fourth. He claims Chickalimmy did him a favor."

"What about the Marshall?"

"Old man Marshall will have to hold on a while yet, 'cause of Chickalimmy, but it won't be long before he closes. Soon as he feathers his nest."

Carrie forced herself to ask, "And the company mine?"

Buzzer swung upside down from a limb. "It's closing, too."

"Did Father say so?"

"He doesn't have to." Buzzer's face was red. He pulled himself upright. "Why do you think he won't buy an icebox? He knows there won't be any ice where we're going."

"Does he know where?"

"Course not, but it'll be a boomer. They always are to start."

His excitement matched Carrie's gloom. They'd have to start in a tent with a wood floor. If the mine was in the desert, lumber would be a long time getting plentiful enough to build houses. Mine shafts came first. There'd be no ice house and no school, though

Carrie was getting too old for school. There'd be even fewer women and children than in String-town.

A stick caught in her hair. Buzzer said, "Wake up, dumb."

"Stop calling me that!"

"Mrs. McPhersen's cat is missing. Willie says she's all cut up over it, thinks the coyotes ate it."

Carrie had too many sorrows of her own to worry about Mrs. McPhersen's Tom.

Buzzer dropped down beside her. "I got a notion the coyotes didn't get it. That maybe that cat's in the Dandy Mine."

"Now who's dumb? There must be a dozen men in the mine every day. If the cat was there, they'd have found it."

"Maybe so, but you might just casual-like mention the cat to Portia and how it might be down in the mine since the Dandy's right back of McPhersen's."

"If you're so blamed sure it's down there, why don't you tell Jed Hopkins so he can look for it?"

"What good will that do?"

"What good will my telling Portia do?"

Buzzer sighed. "Because little Miss Darlingwood's got a mind like a river. You drop in a notion and it runs right out her mouth. Tell me something. How'd you find out the Marshall was closing?"

"What makes you think I did?"

"Come on, Carrie. You can tell me."

"Carrie!" Lonnie came running, followed by a smiling Willie. "Carrie, look what I found."

A little black snake curled around his wrist. Lonnie stroked it gently. "He likes me."

Willie looked sheepish. "It won't hurt him none."

Carrie nodded, her mind on what Buzzer had said. And on what Willie had said about Frank Ainsley wanting to match a cat with a rattlesnake.

Buzzer motioned to Willie who told Lonnie, "We have to get the jar and make a house for him," and led him away.

Carrie told Buzzer, "Frank Ainsley has that cat and I bet Mrs. McPhersen is a member of the Sunday Theosophical Society. You want Chickalimmy to say where the cat is so he'll be right again. Floyd Thaddeus Thatcher, you make me furious!"

She burst into tears.

"What are you crying for?"

"For the crowned heads of Europe," she wailed.

"Now don't tell me you believed in Chickalimmy. You got too much sense."

Too much sense to believe in the crowned heads of Europe, but she had hoped for San Francisco. Hoped and wished so hard that she hadn't let herself think about Chickalimmy's voice. She hadn't let herself know. She wiped her face on her dress sleeve.

"It was you, wasn't it? It was you knocked on the table. How'd you do it?"

"Sneaked through the parlor window with the

clothesline pole. Hid in the hall and just kept jabbing till I hit the table. Ain't easy in the dark, on your hands and knees." He made a face. "It had to hit just when you said I was scared."

"And the scale?" She guessed Frank Ainsley had learned some circus trick for that. She was right.

"Fleas. Frank let some loose inside the dome. Sooner or later one was bound to land on a pan." Buzzer grinned. "You should have seen your face when you ordered him to show and the scale moved. Boy, were you lucky."

"Maybe it wasn't luck. Both times Chickalimmy waited to answer till I called."

If Buzzer was going to call her dumb again he didn't get the chance. Estrella screamed and let loose a flood of Spanish. She came around the house at a run, making a funny sign at Carrie as she passed. Then Lonnie started yelling. When Buzzer and Carrie reached the kitchen, Willie and Lonnie were facing their parents across the table, Lonnie with the snake on his shoulder.

"He likes me," sobbed Lonnie.

"Don't squeeze him," said Willie. "You'll hurt him."

Mrs. Thatcher said to Carrie, "Estrella left. She said the snake was too much."

"But she's already quit," said Willie, "so you ought to let Lonnie keep his friend."

Carrie wanted to pat him on the back. She didn't

remember him ever standing up to anyone before. Now he could deal with Buzzer for Colossus.

"He's right," said Mr. Thatcher. "Getting rid of the snake won't get Estrella back. Isn't the reason she left anyhow."

"I won't have it in the house," said Mother.

"Willie will find a place for it outside, won't you, Willie?" Without waiting for an answer, Mr. Thatcher went back to the sitting room.

Willie looked as if he regretted interfering.

Buzzer took charge. "Come on, you two. We got things to do."

Mrs. Thatcher was already at the sink. "I'll finish the dishes, Carrie. You clean up the dining room."

It was an in-and-out chore which gave Carrie a chance to ask Willie to release her from her promise. She knew the deal Buzzer would make with her for Colossus. She was sure when the time came that Willie would somehow save the spider just as he'd warned Apache Sam and stood up for Lonnie's snake. It was the thinking about it that scared Willie. But he kept looking up with those sad eyes, and Carrie finally promised Buzzer she'd tell Portia about the cat and only about the cat if he'd let Colossus go.

She lay awake a long time listening to the yipping of coyotes. Tears ran into her ears and onto the pillow. She felt the same sadness as when she'd looked at the mummy, only stronger. Some of it was still there when Mother woke her at six o'clock.

When she grumbled about the hour, Mother told her, "You'll get used to it."

"I won't. When I have my own house, I'll get up when I want to."

Mother floured a board to roll out pie dough, baking the day's desserts while the kitchen was at its coolest.

"You sound like Essie," she said.

"And Essie's probably still sleeping." Carrie sliced the peeled potatoes. "Maybe she sleeps till noon."

"Maybe. She won't when the baby comes."

"Essie's having a baby?" No wonder Mother was worried. She'd lost two children herself and hardly a year went by that a mother or baby or both didn't die in Stringtown. Essie, who was going to live like an Indian. Carrie slammed the frying pan on the stove. It wasn't fair. But she couldn't have said what wasn't fair or why she was crying again.

Mother patted her shoulder. "Don't worry. She'll be all right."

Carrie wasn't sure it was Essie she'd been crying for. She brooded through breakfast and drying the dishes. She was making the beds, still in a gray mood, when Portia pounded up the stairs and dropped onto Lonnie's rumpled bed.

"I'm going to San Francisco," she announced.

Carrie pushed her out of the way.

Portia added, "We leave tomorrow."

"You can't!"

"Mama says Apaches are less of a risk than the atmosphere of Stringtown. She means Chickalimmy. She says appearing at the Sunday Theosophical Society is akin to professional acting."

Carrie had often heard from Portia that professional actresses were not ladies and no actor was socially accepted. "But she told Mrs. Smedley you could go."

"No, I told her. Mama was upstairs with a cold compress so I talked to Mrs. Smedley. Mama didn't know until dinner. She made a terrible fuss."

"I guess she figures it was my fault."

In a way it was. Buzzer was her brother and the Rough-n-Ready had been her idea. But Portia had brought up séances and done all the swooning and captured-by-Chickalimmy stuff. Now she was going off and leaving it all to Carrie because it wasn't lady-like.

"There's more," Portia told her. "I'm not coming back. Papa says prospects are declining here so we're staying in California."

Carrie nodded. She couldn't think of anything Portia would want to hear. They walked downstairs in silence. Carrie opened the front door.

Portia said, "Will you come down to the stage and see me off?"

Other years, Carrie had been asked to dinner the night before Portia left. "I won't have time. Estrella quit."

"I guess this is good-by then."

"I guess so."

They stood awkwardly a moment, then Portia started across the porch. Carrie closed the door quietly, as a lady should. Mrs. Dollingwood couldn't have done it better. Then she stomped through the house, fighting back tears.

"I'll help carry the potatoes out," said Mother. "Now what's the matter?"

"Portia's moving to San Francisco so she can be a lady and live like one of her magazine stories."

Mother smiled and filled a pan with water. "She'll get married like everyone else. Her life won't be so different."

Carrie didn't believe it. Portia's life was already different. It was Carrie who'd be the same, like Mother, like Essie. She sat on the steps and peeled what she figured was her millionth potato.

All three boys climbed past her carrying empty canning jars. Willie beamed.

"No more matches," he told Carrie. "Buzzer says he has more important business."

Lonnie struggled with a jar under each arm. Carrie boosted him up the steps.

"What are you doing with those?" she asked him.

"Buzzer says I got to pay him back 'cause he helped me fix a place for Horse."

"I thought you had a snake."

"That's his name. Horse."

On their way out for another load Carrie stopped Buzzer. "I didn't tell Portia about the cat. She's leaving for San Francisco tomorrow and she's never coming back."

Buzzer didn't take long to think about it. "That's all right. You can do Chickalimmy. Frank says you've got more sense anyhow. Just be sure Chickalimmy tells about Mrs. McPhersen's cat."

"No. It's dishonest."

"Why? You aren't telling lies."

And when it came to dishonesty, what about Portia's grand swoons? Carrie jabbed at the potato eyes. "It isn't ladylike."

"Who cares? It makes money. Lots of money if it's done right. Frank can help us. He says it isn't too different from a circus."

"Hurry up, Buzzer." Lonnie danced in the yard. "I got to feed Horse."

Buzzer waved to him. "You can do it, Carrie. You want Mrs. McPhersen to find her cat, don't you?"

Carrie watched him cross the yard and picked up another potato. "One million and one."

She bet Madame Batashka never peeled potatoes. She probably slept until noon and then rode down Market Street in a carriage. Not that Carrie intended to become a spiritist. But it did sound as if Mrs. McPhersen wasn't going to get her cat unless Chickalimmy spoke. And what about Geronimo? Nobody would listen to Willie or Apache Sam, but if Chickalimmy said something, they'd believe.

And how did she know there wasn't a Chicka-limmy? Buzzer had hit the table with a pole and Frank Ainsley had let loose some fleas, but both times nothing had happened until Carrie spoke. Maybe it wasn't just luck.

One thing was certain. If Chickalimmy spoke to the Sunday Theosophical Society he'd help General Crook and make an old lady happy. Just once wouldn't hurt, not if she was helping people. And if she could do it.

Carrie placed knife and potato on the step beside her, held out her hands and closed her eyes.

"My name is Chickalimmy," she whispered. "Hear me! I speak true. Geronimo is in Mexico. Chihuahua raids here."

Mother was right. All she had to do was put her mind to it.

About the Author

Betty Baker has done a bit of everything—from working as a dental assistant to assembling xylophones in a toy factory—but her main interests are books, people and travel. Her special interest in children's books began when her son, Christopher, was young, and in 1962 her first book, the popular *Little Runner of the Longhouse*, was published for beginning readers. Since that time she has written more than a dozen notable books, nonfiction as well as fiction, for young people of varying ages.

Born in Pennsylvania, Miss Baker has lived in Arizona for many years and most of her books deal with the Southwest and with the Indians of that area. She was for five years editor of *The Roundup*, the monthly magazine of the Western Writers of America.

She has won the Western Heritage Award for the outstanding Western juvenile book twice: in 1963 for *Killer-of-Death* and in 1970 for *And One Was a Wooden Indian*. In 1967 she received the Spur Award of the Western Writers of America for *The Dunderhead War*.

Betty Baker's other books include *At the Center of the World*, *A Stranger and Afraid*, *Do Not Annoy the Indians*, *Walk the World's Rim*, *The Shaman's Last Raid* and *The Pig War*.